Am I Clear Now?

In the room's dim light, Slocum checked the loads in his .44 and then holstered it. *Better go face these devils, whoever they are.* When the door opened, they all went for their gun butts.

"Hold your fire," McKee said. "This is my partner, Slocum. Slocum, meet John King and his associates."

King, a portly man in a dark oilskin duster, pulled the coat back and exposed an ivory-handled Colt with a steer head carved on it. Nickel plated, too.

"Maybe you know where that slinking Wolf Ripley's at?"

"He may be going to sprout daisies come the spring thaw."

"How is that?"

"I found his woman about two months or so back in a dust storm. I brought her here and she had no idea where he ended up. They'd come under attack and she lit out."

"She's lying to cover for the sumbitch," King swore.

Slocum shook his head. "She doesn't know where he's at. Am I clear enough?"

"You covering for some red whore?"

"Listen, King, you call her nothing but 'ma'am' or I'll blow you to kingdom come."

King sniffed out his nose.

That was all it took. Slocum drew and fired at him. King's left hand shot to his ear, and he screamed, "You shot me."

"You want the other one notched?"

JAKE LOGAN

SLOCUM AND THE SANTA FE SISTERS

JOVE BOOKS, NEW YORK

THE BERKLEY PUBLISHING GROUP
Published by the Penguin Group
Penguin Group (USA) Inc.
375 Hudson Street, New York, New York 10014, USA

USA / Canada / UK / Ireland / Australia / New Zealand / India / South Africa / China

Penguin Books Ltd., Registered Offices: 80 Strand, London WC2R 0RL, England
For more information about the Penguin Group visit penguin.com

SLOCUM AND THE SANTA FE SISTERS

A Jove Book / published by arrangement with the author

Jove Books are published by The Berkley Publishing Group.
JOVE® is a registered trademark of Penguin Group (USA) Inc.
The "J" design is a trademark of Penguin Group (USA) Inc.

For information, address: The Berkley Publishing Group,
a division of Penguin Group (USA) Inc.,
375 Hudson Street, New York, New York 10014.

ISBN: 978-0-515-15312-5

PUBLISHING HISTORY
Jove mass-market edition / April 2013

PRINTED IN THE UNITED STATES OF AMERICA

10 9 8 7 6 5 4 3 2 1

Cover illustration by Sergio Giovine.

ALWAYS LEARNING   **PEARSON**

1

The wind hollered without a break for his ears. There was no escaping its screaming whine. In the blurry brown daylight, hard-driving grit slashed at his eyes and the exposed facial features above his tightly tied kerchief mask. Even with his mouth covered by the thick cloth, he still tasted diamond-like grains of grit riding on the surface of his teeth. With his spurs constantly gouging the bay horse to wade on into the force of the Texas dry hurricane, John Slocum huddled in his saddle under a flapping wool blanket he used for warmth. He knew the bay and his packhorse had made little progress in his day-long attempt to reach Colonel Gill McKee's Fort Contention out on Cap Rock.

He spotted, in the storm, a small huddled procession heading toward him. Two heavily loaded burros and a small figure leaning into the wind pulling them to follow. They had to be lost. He reined the bay in their direction. When he reached them, the person doing the leading turned her head away from the wind, and he could make out the face of a young Indian woman.

He dismounted and used the downwind side of his horse to block some of the force.

"Are you lost?" he shouted over the howling wind.

She nodded. "Look for Wolf," she called back.

"Who's he?"

"Sells whiskey."

"Your man?" Even his horse as a defense didn't break much of the entire strength of the blast they were under. She nodded to his question.

"This crazy weather will settle in a day or so. We need to get under a bluff."

"Where?" She shook her head like that was impossible.

Her short-cut hair kept blowing around on her face and into her eyes, forcing her to push it back with both hands. Sometime in the past, her thin nose had been broken and had healed with a slight, but not unattractive, crookedness. The thin copper lips were straight, serious lines, and she did not crack even a small smile. But the round dark brown pupils showed the fear she held inside for the situation that they were in as well as her wariness toward the tall stranger.

"How long has he been gone?"

She held up two fingers.

"Two days?"

She nodded.

He pulled the brim of his hat down to better secure it. "You have any water?"

"Not much."

He took the large canteen from his saddle horn and took the lid off it. She gave him the burros' lead ropes to hold, held the canteen up with both hands, and sipped from it slowly, then gave it back.

"Muchas gracias, señor." One-handed, she brought the blanket back over her head and tried to fix her hair to see again. "Where can we go?"

"If I knew that, I'd be there. This wind is driving me

crazy. Would you like some jerky?" Hell, if she hadn't had any water, she'd probably not eaten anything either.

She agreed with a nod and he got some out of his saddlebags. With her back against the bay's side, she nodded her approval and began to chew on the small dark slab of dried beef.

"Where are you going?" she asked between bites.

"McKee's Fort Contention."

"Is it close?" Her look at him turned serious.

"It should be, but I'm afraid I might have ridden by it."

Pushing her hair aside, she wearily agreed. "You might have."

"What's on the burros?"

She shook her head in disgust. "Only whiskey."

"This damn wind has to go down—sometime. Let's stay here and maybe it will let up."

"I only have this blanket." She indicated the one flapping over her head.

He nodded. "I have a small canvas tent and some stakes. We can hobble the animals. Stake the tent down and get under it. It won't make much of a shelter, but we can be out of the damn wind."

She nodded again, as if anything was better than being out in that infernal blast. Slocum left her to hold the horses and unloaded the tent. The wind nearly tore it away from him. With a short-handled farrier hammer, he drove the stakes down and then undid the tent. The wind's force would not let him tie it on those pegs. He used the two upright short poles and then the gale wouldn't let him hold down the other side and drive in those pegs, but eventually he managed to get it set up.

They hobbled the animals with their tails turned into the wind and also tied their leads together. He brought in the canteen, his saddlebags, and his bedroll. The woman quickly rolled it out to sit on while gale forces worked hard on the small tent sides. Slocum crawled in to join her. The ends were tied down securely, and as he lay down on the bedroll, he thought he had escaped to a new land.

He removed his boots and gun belt, but with no appetite for food, he told the woman to help herself. She did so in the darkness. He crawled under the blankets, spreading his cover blanket over the others. Finally on his back under the covers, he thanked God for this small sanctuary.

"When you get through eating, crawl in."

She nodded, and he soon was asleep. Sometime in the night, he awoke. What was wrong? No wind. But his breath came out in big steamy clouds in the near darkness. He got up carefully after feeling for the woman's small body, not under his covers but wrapped in her own blanket close by. He untied the tent end by feel. Open at last, he stared out at a blanket of ghostly white carpeting the ground. Large flakes were falling so he went back inside and pulled his boots on.

He came outside again and emptied his bladder behind a rock. The flakes settled and melted on his face as he buttoned his fly and returned to the tent. What next?

"Plenty of snow," she said, peering out of the tent at the new sight.

"Plenty, but the wind's died down, thank God."

"Sí." She nodded her head, and he crawled past her to get inside. Then she went out, for the same purpose, he figured.

What was her name? He would ask her when she came back. The name "Wolf" meant nothing to him. There were lots of whiskey traders out there in vacant West Texas. They had to avoid local law and rangers as well as some U.S. marshals who wanted to collect federal taxes on their wares of snake bite medicine. Most of these peddlers were more Injun than white and lived on the border of civilization, making money selling arms and firewater to the renegades. Tougher than most, they lived on a thin line the savages walked beyond the arm of the law.

The woman crawled back inside the dark tent on her hands and knees.

"What's your name?" he asked.

"What does he call me?"

He nodded. "That or what you like to be called."

"He calls me Bitch."

"What do your people call you?"

"Puta."

"Let's try again." He discovered by bowing his head, he could sit up on the bedroll in the darkness. "What were you called as a girl?"

"My name was Julie Henry on the reservation registration. The government gave me that name."

"Will I call you Julie?" He saw her smile for the first time in the faint light. "How old are you?"

"Maybe twenty." She turned up her palms, sitting facing him in the dim starlight.

"I was born on the reservation in the mountains. When I was put on the rolls, I was, they said, five. I did not understand the white man's way of such things. Later I was married to a Navajo man and he was murdered by his enemies. Because he died, the leader said I had encouraged them to kill him." She shook her head to deny that. "So they sold me to a trader as a slave. He beat me. I ran away and lived like an animal in a cave. Wolf found me and took me along."

"He did not beat you."

She held one finger up. "He beat me one time. That night I woke him up and held his manhood in one hand and his sharp skinning knife in my other. I told him, 'You beat me again, I will cut it off while you sleep.' He never beat me again."

"Julie, I damn sure won't beat you."

She giggled. Indian women did not laugh but they giggled over funny things. She was no inexperienced teenager; she had learned survival.

He needed to figure out some things at first light. How

far away were they from McKee's Fort? That, in this trace-less land, would be hard to figure out, but otherwise they'd come to some road that wagon trains took heading west. Be hard to miss those tracks. The Comanche were in winter quarters in Palo Duro Canyon, no doubt hiding from the Army.

He'd been there once. Best-kept secret in the world. The well-watered canyon was several hundred feet below the rim of the rest of the high plains country. Had lots of cedars for firewood, grass for their ponies, a free-flowing creek, plenty of game, and a much better climate than up on Cap Rock. It was only a matter of time until the Army found them there and ended that paradise for the tough horsemen. The Cheyenne also wintered there and had a peace agreement with the Comanche.

Strange how the two of them could be a few or a hundred miles from McKee's place. Slocum thought his course had been right until the dust storm came. Where was her man? How did they get separated? Was she running away from him? No way to know. She might tell him later. Then again, she might not.

2

They rode north for two days, their only source of water some puddles of melted snow. Then Slocum spotted McKee's tall flagstaff on a far rise. Riding double behind Slocum, Julie leaned forward as he pointed it out to her.

"Who is he?"

"A crazy old mountain man who trapped beavers fifty years ago in the Rockies. He hates civilization and calls this his land. He has several common-law Indian wives and some Mexicans who work for him."

She leaned forward and made a face at him. "Why you go there?"

"No one bothers me there."

He saw her nod to indicate that she understood.

She'd proved to be his near-silent companion the entire trip. At times she'd grasped his canvas coat to catch her balance or she'd stretched a stiff leg forward and lightly bumped one of his. They'd had only some jerky and dry cheese with crackers to eat. Even the occasional jackrabbits that popped up looked too skinny to shoot for meat, and the cold had driven the snakes into hibernation. He had not missed eating them, even though snake wasn't half bad when you were hungry enough.

He settled down riding toward his goal at last. With a firm grip, he clasped Julie's thin leg. "We can sleep together in a bed tonight."

"If you wish me to."

"Of course, if you don't want to, you don't have to."

She put her hand over his. "I thought after two days together that you didn't like Indian women."

"Whoa, horse!" he shouted. The horse stopped, dropped his head, and pulled up the sparse snow-clogged brown vegetation for a few bites.

Twisting around in the saddle, he looked her directly in the eye. "Did I say that?"

She giggled. "Two nights I waited but you never touched me."

He reined up the horse again. "I was trying to get us up here."

"You did a fine job of that."

"Thanks. Then we can celebrate tonight?"

She hugged him. "I will take a bath."

"Let's both get cleaned up."

"Does McKee have enough water for that?"

"I believe he does. Let's go, horse. We've got a big night planned. She and I are going to celebrate tonight." He let out a rebel yell that shattered the silence of the open country. Then he said over his shoulder to her, "We better watch Wolf's liquor at this place. Desperate dry men who come by are always looking for free whiskey."

She leaned forward and asked, "Do you drink?"

"Not much, darling."

"He would be mad when he finds me and it is all gone."

"Figure he's alive?"

She laughed. "Wolf is still alive. He has just not found us yet."

"Well, he owes me for finding you."

She poked him in the back. "I found you."

"Whatever you say, darlin'."

They rode on up to the flag that McKee had made some-where, and it showed a bull buffalo and a great bear fight-ing. He called it the "Where All Hell Broke Loose" flag.

When the black Indian dogs discovered them coming and began barking, some squaws came out first. They used their hands to shade their eyes from the glare to see who it was. Then armed with a rifle and wearing buckskins, the big man himself came out to observe the latest invaders.

"Well, I'll be fiddle-damned," he shouted. "It's ole roo-tin'-tootin' Slocum come to see us, women. We better get cooking. He ain't ate in a week, I bet. Get down here. What're you doing, peddling whiskey?"

"No, these are Julie Henry's burros and a trader named Wolf's whiskey. They got separated back a ways and she hasn't seen him in four days."

"I bet sure as hell that he finds you."

"I don't care, except he owes me some for saving that whiskey and his woman in a damn dust storm." Slocum threw his leg over the horn, slid off the horse, and shook the man's hand.

"By God, you're a sight for sore eyes, Slocum. Howdy, ma'am." He doffed his big felt hat for her. "Welcome to Fort Contention."

Slocum caught and set Julie down. "We'll put the whis-key in Mac's warehouse, and it will be safe there."

"You can bet your squaw boots it'll be in there when you want it." He spun around to face Slocum. "And where in the hell've you been?"

"I spent some time over in Silver City, then went down to see Virgil Earp at Tombstone."

"I always liked him. The other one's there, huh?"

"Doc's still drinking but his lungs won't last much longer."

"He always was a horse's ass in my book. Virgil I could

stand, but the rest of them never amounted to much. What're they doing down there?"

"Doing some law work and trying to get rich. They've got a gaming concession in a saloon."

"They got whores, too."

"Doc's got one. Big Nose Kate."

"Oh God, I recall her from Dodge. Meaner than a rattle-snake." McKee shook his head.

"We'll unlock the storeroom and put the whiskey inside." Slocum looked around. He didn't see any stray horses so there must not have been any other visitors there at that time.

"Take them jasshonkeys behind the main building. I'll give the keys to my women and they'll help you unload them," he said to Julie. "I'll borrow Slocum here, and you can join us in the store when you get the whiskey unloaded. Put them donkeys in a pen by themselves. We'll see you when you're done."

Julie nodded.

"The boss of my crew is the tall woman. Willow's her name," he said after her.

With a nod, Julie led the burros off, and a short Mexican boy took Slocum's mount and the packhorse.

"Put his saddle and pack stuff in the Jefferson Davis House," McKee told the boy. "It's the best guest quarters on Cap Rock. Build a fire in there for him and have them heat some water for their baths. He'll want one, I know."

"So will she."

"Tell 'em two bathers, savvy, hombre?"

"Sí, señor." The boy led off the two horses. Julie already had taken the burros around in back.

They went in and sat down at a round table with a scarred top. Slocum held up his hand to stop McKee when he raised a small jug to fill a glass for him. "I'm not drinking right now."

"Hell, did you go turn preacher on me?"

"No, I'm just not drinking right now. It's been a helluva haul to get out here. I want to rest up some."

"You seen Slim Jenkins or Rowdy Bill?"

"Rowdy Bill I heard fell down the stairs in a Socorro, Texas, whorehouse and broke his neck last year. They said the whores cried for a week over their loss. The undertaker told me why. He said Rowdy had a dick as big as a stud horse's even after he was dead three days."

"He could make all them whores smile." McKee shook his head and then downed a big swig of wild cat piss from his glass. "Here's to Rowdy, my old friend, who fell down the whorehouse—what rhymes with 'friend'—oh, fell down the stairs in the end. With a dick bigger than a horse, he had no money, of course. But he screwed them all and made his life a ball. Ole Saint Peter gave him his call when he came through them gates, and back on earth, all them gals showed their hates at the death of their greatest man of all."

"You call that the 'Ode to Rowdy'?"

"Sorry I wasn't there at his funeral, or I could've told them of the time I seed him up on the Green River at Rendezvous, when he screwed four squaws in a row. When he finished with one, he went on to the next. He was better than any stallion I ever seed."

Slocum nodded. "They said he was eighty-two when he died and could still do three in a row."

"I don't doubt it. Last time we got drunk together, I think he had four gals in one night."

"Sounds like something you'd do, McKee."

"Yup. And no one can do it like I did. I left Saint Louie right after Lewis and Clark did. I always wanted to seduce that woman who went with them. Her name was Sacagawea. Married to some Frenchman and she had a baby. Man, to a kid of fourteen, she was like a goddess.

"I seen her in the Mandan camp. Man, what a woman. She carried herself like royalty and her tits held out that beaded elk skin dress. I got a hard-on just watching her walk by me."

"You liked them two guys?"

"I really liked Captain Clark—he was a man's man. Meriwether was always looking at things and writing 'em down like a schoolmarm. I traveled with them for a while."

"You've lived a helluva life," Slocum said as Julie joined them.

She said, "They have brought hot water to our cabin."

"Well, I better go get a bath. Thanks for your hospitality." He rose and shook McKee's hand. "We'll talk more later."

McKee nodded at both of them. "Don't you two go do what I'd liked to do right now."

Then he laughed aloud.

"I didn't want the water to get cold," Julia said, hurrying beside Slocum as they crossed the snowy yard toward their guest house. It was actually a jacal, a small thatched hut with walls made from upright poles joined together with clay. The flaming sun was setting in the west on another short, cold, wintery day.

"No, I was ready for a bath. Thanks for coming for me."

She smiled, pleased by his answer. "I am, too."

As soon as they were in their jacal, Slocum undressed quickly, then climbed into the half barrel of steaming water and began soaping himself. Julia used a long-handled brush on his back and he laughed. Then she shed her clothing and he saw her small pear-shaped breasts, which shook as she worked naked on him with a soapy rag. At last, holding his white-lathered dick in her hand, she nodded in approval at the sight of it, then she released it.

With a smile, she leaned over, reaching into the barrel to gently heft his balls in her palm. "I am glad you are here."

"Do you miss Wolf?"

She shook her head, as if disgusted. Then she took the

pail of water, stood on a chair, and poured it over Slocum's head to rinse him. He stepped out and she began to vigorously dry him off with sack towels. Dry, he lifted her under the arms and put her in the barrel. He kissed a pointed nipple as it went by his mouth and brought a genuine smile to her face. She quickly washed and nodded to him for the last rinse pail. He doused her, then lifted her out and kissed her on the mouth.

Her dark eyes flew open, and she threw her arms around his neck and really kissed him back. He could hardly wait to get her dry. After she was dry enough, he carried her to his bedroll, which she'd already spread on the bed, and laid her on it. The fire in the corner fireplace crackled and consumed a mixture of mesquite and oak logs. Its warmth spread over their exposed skin and he kissed her small, hard nipples. Slowly his mouth traced a line down her flat belly until his lips reached the mound of pubic hair. Sighing, she spread her short legs wide apart for him.

When he kissed the lips of her vagina, she cried out loud and pulled hard on him to get him to climb on top of her. But he made her wait, licking and teasing her into a blazing flame of wantonness. His lashing tongue destroyed her sanity and he found her desperate for his growing erection, which he soon drove into her slick wetness. She moaned and tossed her head on the blanket underneath him.

Her fingernails dug into the flesh on his back, and her loud cries filled the room. After a long series of shudders, she came, and her juices flooded over his dick and balls. She lay back, limp, but he began to thrust inside her again, watching her recover then suddenly come a second time. He drove his swollen dick as deep as it would go into her. With the pressure rising in his tubes, he let go with a cannon shot of seminal fluid. She screamed out her pleasure as he filled her to the brim. When he had fully emptied himself inside her, they both lay still, exhausted and satisfied.

They rested there for a long time, connected, in a nap. Long after sundown, they awoke in the dark room, with only the dying fire's light dancing off her smooth copper face. This time they had more controlled sex.

Later that night, McKee's three Mexican helpers returned with a fresh-killed buffalo carcass in a carreta, which squeaked so loud it woke Slocum up a half hour before it ever reached the fort. He dressed and went outside to see. Julie got up, did the same, and soon found him by the carreta.

"He's a big bull," he pointed out to her. The hide from his large set of balls had been saved to shrink-wrap on a saddle horn. Dried, it would make dally roping easier. Light came from the open back door of the large kitchen as two squaws in the carreta used a hatchet and handsaw to butcher the carcass into more manageable pieces. Other women carried large portions of the cut-up meat inside to work them over in there. The sour smell of guts along with the copper flavor of blood were on Slocum's tongue as everyone huffed out steamy clouds of breath while they worked to break down the carcass.

A tall Indian woman brought some sliced fried liver on a tin plate for them to eat.

Slocum thanked her, and they began to enjoy the strong-tasting hot strips, feeding each other with their fingers. As the big squaw was about to go through the lighted doorway, he shouted after her, "Thank you."

She waved and went back to finish her task.

"I can help her," Julie said, then left Slocum to go inside to find the tall woman.

The night wind was cold, but the fried liver filled his guts and warmed him. Julie brought him a tin cup of steaming coffee and he thanked her. Savoring the richness on his tongue, he listened to the three men's Spanish bragging about killing the bull with two shots from a Sharps .50-caliber rifle.

In his days spent as a hunter, Slocum had shot lots of them. He made one shot do. If the buffalo discovered someone was shooting at them, they fled. Any wounded bawling buffalo would stampede. The object was to keep them in the gun's range and pick them off one at a time while they grazed or switched pesky biting flies with their small tails. His largest count was fifty-two, all falling dead in a small pattern and not one stampede. But the days of such wild commercial hunting were over. The buffalo were now found only in small scattered herds. In a few years they'd all be gone.

At last, Slocum went back to their small jacal to catch some more sleep. Julie was busy working with McKee's women and didn't appear to care. He undressed down to his long-handle underwear, banked the fire in the fireplace, and climbed under the covers. In the bed, he reached down and felt his half-full erection. Oh well, in the morning he'd use it again. Amused by his thoughts of the excitement he'd given her, he soon went back to sleep.

Before dawn Slocum arose, pulled on his boots, and went outside in the hard rush of air full of cold sleet striking his cheek. He emptied his bladder on the lee side of the adobe building. Back inside, in the orange light from the fireplace, he slipped back into bed and discovered Julie's naked form under the covers. He worked his way carefully, trying not to wake her, until he was up against her bare ass. His fingers were at last warm enough to probe her.

Then gently he rolled her over on her back under the covers. On his side next to her, he began to gently probe her pussy with his fingers. Very slow and easy. She soon split her legs farther apart for him and moaned. Her clitoris grew harder as the tip of his thumb stirred her sexuality. Her heartbeat and breath increased as his dick began to swell. He unbuttoned the lower portion of his long johns so his privates were exposed to the outside.

Watching her tan face in the orange glare of the fire, he

noted that her eyes never cracked open. He rose on his knees and she made a place for him between her short legs. On top of her, he moved forward to slip the head of his cock into the wet lips of her vagina, only inches inside her sacred cavity.

Slowly he eased it in a short ways then he backed it out. The sharp point of her erect clit scratched the hard tender head each time it went in and out. When he plunged into her again, she raised her hips to meet him, and her small hands clutched the cheeks of his ass, pushing him in deeper. Her legs wrapped around his, and they fell into a fast rhythmic pattern of pumping into her moist, tight pussy.

Out of breath, she smiled in the dim light. "After the last few years of being with Wolf, who is small, you are real big treat to me."

Then she lifted her hips off the mattress again and humped him furiously toward the end. They went on forever, but finally she began shuddering and clamping down on him and he came in a thunderous ejection of hot seminal fluid. Finally they collapsed in a blinding finish of wet kisses.

He closed his eyes, then he lay back down beside her and cupped a rock-hard teacup breast. What a wonderful treasure he'd found in a severe West Texas dust storm.

The next day, the low cloud cover moved stiffly northeast over Cap Rock. It spit some snow, and at midday a band of Comanche came to trade. They brought four women with them. That meant they weren't a war party. Still, Slocum had never felt completely comfortable about the crooked-legged warriors who rode horses wherever they went.

These men had no respect for their women, who lived a harsh slave's role. He recalled a chief down in West Texas who forced a white captive woman to blow his dick in front of some traders to show how he treated her. For Slocum, it was a gruesome sight to endure. These four females had

had their hair slashed off short by knives and wore rags so they would not appeal to other men.

He knew old mountain men like McKee never took a Comanche woman for a bride. They lived in such a dry land they never took baths, and most of the white men out there avoided their smelly camps and rode upwind from the old ones. On Slocum's trips with Comancheros, he learned lots about the whole stinking business of the Comanche lifestyle.

Wrapped in blankets, the band sat on the cold ground around a large fire and tried to trade with McKee. Slocum and Julie walked past them and entered the post to get some breakfast. The tall Indian woman, Willow, met them and invited them into the kitchen, which smelled of cooking food.

She brought him some coffee and her a cup of cocoa, which made her smile.

"Are they doing anything out there?" the tall one asked him.

"Talking," Slocum said.

"They said when they got here that they have two white captives who belonged to a rich man in Santa Fe. That he would pay a big price for them."

Julie wrinkled her nose at him like she didn't believe that. "They are all such big liars and smell like they've never wiped their asses."

Slocum chuckled at his woman's words and watched her pinch her nose. "They are big liars," Julie said again before taking another sip of her hot chocolate.

"Do you want some roasted buffalo and fry bread?" Willow asked.

"Sounds wonderful," Slocum said and turned as McKee came in the door, allowing some cold air inside with him.

"How's it going out there?" Slocum asked.

"Like all trading with them bastards. Red Bear has two girls out there. He took them off a stage he says and wants to sell them. I can't hardly stand for any white girl to be in their grasp, and by now they're both probably pregnant."

"Have you seen them?"

"No, they're holding 'em out at some camp they have over the hill."

"How much do they want for them?"

"Plenty. I won't pay 'em that much."

Slocum nodded. "What can I do?"

"Eat some breakfast. I will, too, Willow," he said to the woman. "They can think on what I offered and go get those white girls if they accept it."

"I saw four women were with them when they rode in," Slocum offered. "I looked them over."

"That's not the girls they want to trade. Two of those are Mexican women. No doubt captured in raids they made in Mexico, but they are filthy stinking slave-wives, too."

Willow brought them heaping plates of browned rich-smelling meat and puffy hot fry bread. Then more coffee for the men and chocolate for Julie.

Between bites, Slocum asked him what they wanted for the captives.

"Oh, the usual. Whiskey, sugar, cornmeal, and gunpowder. I have plenty of whiskey and cornmeal. Maybe a couple sacks of sugar and a keg of gunpowder. They can't get any more than that anywhere out here for those girls. But I want to see them and be certain that they are who he says they are. These people lie like a dog barks—all the time."

They all laughed and enjoyed their breakfast.

When they'd finished, McKee asked Slocum to join him. "Come along with me. We'll see who they have as captives."

Slocum agreed, squeezed Julie's shoulder, and told her he'd be back. He buttoned up his blanket-lined canvas coat and followed the older man out the door into the mouth of winter.

McKee introduced Slocum as his best friend to the seated Indians, and Red Bear showed them where to take a place beside him.

"What does trader want?" Red Bear asked in halting English.

"The two hostages. I must talk to them."

Red Bear motioned to a woman outside the circle and spoke in guttural words to her.

"He said go get them," McKee told Slocum.

In turn, McKee nodded.

The two women set out for them.

Several Indians pointed at Slocum and talked, nodding their heads about something. It did not look hostile, but he was unsure about their meaning.

Red Bear finally spoke to him. "They say you came with Comacheros one time."

"Yes, I came three times when I lived among them in New Mexico."

Red Bear was a big man by these people's standards. Most of the men were hardly over five feet and the women even shorter. He'd never met Red Bear before, but he knew much about the Comanches from his trading experiences the West. According to history, these people came from the North. They were Shoshone people who lived on mountain goats and had been pushed by the Crows into the Rockies, where existence was hard. Then the Sioux came from the northern woods and drove the Crow off the buffalo plains.

A band of Shoshone warriors came south, found the Spanish horse, and became a tough cavalry. They were powerful enough to drive the eastern Apaches off the plains. This was a warrior society, and if you could not ride, fight, and hunt, you chose suicide or being murdered. They simply eliminated the old women, the barren, and crippled ones or abandoned them to die by themselves. They had no religion and did no ceremonial dances, but they did dance or stomp as a social event. Men like McKee who knew the Shoshone language could speak with them. Many of those women left their tribes and became the "wives" of the early trappers.

A Cherokee woman once told Slocum why so many of their women married the Scots-Irish traders. She smiled and said, "The traders all had iron pots to cook in instead of skin ones."

It made good sense.

Slocum sat beside McKee as the Comanche argued around their circle about the poor offer McKee had made for the two women they held. How they could take them to New Mexico and get a chest of gold for them.

McKee said something in Comanche to counter their argument and caused them to laugh. He leaned over and spoke to Slocum. "I told them a soldier would put hot bullets up their asses if they went over there."

Slocum agreed. "When will they decide about this trade?"

"Oh, they don't have anything else to do. Red Bear said they'd all fucked the four women with them and wanted to go back to their home camp for some better pickings."

"Probably the captives want the same thing. To get away from those bastards."

McKee agreed.

Red Bear finally spoke. "You are cheating us. These are good princesses. Maybe when you see them, you will give twice as much."

The chief and the rest of them tore out small dead blades of buffalo grass and threw them up to see the wind's direction. Another hour passed. A McKee Mexican brought more logs for their fire. The air had not warmed hardly a degree since sunup. Gloomy clouds still passed over them.

The two captives arrived, wrapped in thin blankets and joined with heavy ropes tied around their necks. Hair in braids, they wore blank expressions on their faces, and when they got before Red Bear, the two of them were stripped of their blankets. Naked in the cold wind, they huddled for warmth, but one of the Comanche squaws prodded them apart with a quirt and motioned for them to stand straight.

Neither of the teenagers was pretty. They were white women, with small tits, the broad shoulders of a man, and wide hips with dark pubic hair in their crotches. One girl's belly was visibly pregnant while the other's was firm and flat.

"Tell them your name," Red Bear commanded.

"Elania Proctor," the taller of the two girls said. "Our father is a prominent storekeeper in Santa Fe. He is rich and I swear he will pay a thousand dollars in gold for us. This is my sister, her name is Katrina. She has not spoken in many days—weeks—since they kidnapped us." She shivered violently.

"You know of such a man?" McKee asked Slocum.

"Yes, Proctor has a big mercantile store a block off the square."

"Cover them up," McKee said to Red Bear. "I cannot get a nickel for a frozen hostage. Send them inside the store."

Slocum never made a sign or said a word, only sat hard-eyed beside McKee and waited, but he obviously also wanted them out of the cold.

"Good," Red Bear said. "We will trade and then go back to our own camp."

McKee motioned to the girls, who had both begun to cry as they wrapped their blankets around themselves again to hide their nakedness and then stumbled to the doorway that Willow held open for them.

One Comanche buck spoke in English to Slocum as they started to leave. "That one talks too much," he said, pointing to Elania. "The other one only cries."

Slocum nodded as if he were grateful for that information. "Thanks."

Inside he joined Julie standing at the fireplace. Neither

Willow nor the captives were in the store. He glanced around.

"Willow took them to fit them into some clothing. Those men are bastards to do that to them," Julie said under her breath. "Are they gone?"

"For now."

"I would stick a big branch up that chief's ass and break it off so he could not get it out."

He chuckled. "I can tell you don't like them."

She poked him in the muscle-ribbed gut with her flat hand.

"I hate them. Those Indians wanted to make a showing of their power. I once asked for a white woman they held, and this chief went over, tore back his breechcloth, and made her suck him off until he came."

"He must have been this Red Bear's brother."

"It was very bad."

"I can see that it must have been. Can we go back to bed now for something quick before we're needed to help out around here?"

"Absolutely." She poked him in the gut and giggled. "You are a big man, Slocum. How long can we stay here?"

"Until he runs us off."

"What can we do until spring?"

"We can play in bed."

"Oh, that will be fun."

"If you need us, we'll be at the jacal," he called over his shoulder to McKee.

"Sure enough. Take your time."

Slocum laughed and they went back to the small dwelling. He considered the shifting of snow on the wind. It might really pile up if it ever started snowing in a serious fashion. Oh well, with Julie's sweet body to enjoy and McKee's hosting them, he was well provided for.

Unless some traveling merchant came along, McKee would probably want him to take those two females to

Santa Fe and try to collect a large reward from their father. But Slocum wasn't volunteering for the job.

He closed and bolted the door of the jacal after they'd come in from the cold. Julie knelt down and started rebuilding the fire.

He closed his eyes and savored his warm paradise.

3

While Julie rested, Slocum repaired his saddle and packs and thoroughly cleaned his two pistols and Winchester rifle. One was a .30-caliber Colt he kept as a hideaway gun. It was a cap and ball weapon. The dusting of snow melted when the sun came out, but the snow returned in a few days to blanket Cap Rock in a day-and-night-long blizzard. The snow was over a foot deep, and McKee was pacing the floor, concerned about his helpers, who were out hunting for meat and had not come back the night before.

"I'll ride out and find them," Slocum said, "if they don't come in today."

"I hate for you to have to do that," McKee said.

Slocum dismissed his concern. "No problem."

"Thanks. You are a true friend."

"No, I'm a leech waiting for spring."

McKee laughed. "A better one I don't know. You are such good company, I enjoy talking with you about the old days. This snow reminds me of another bad winter. I was in Montana in the Rockies living in a cave with a Sioux woman after a grizzly attack about sent me to hell. I'd've

24

been in bad shape if she hadn't nursed me back to health. I was sure grateful to her and promised her I'd buy her lots of things.

"Well, we had three mules loaded with good furs. And more cached down south I planned to pick up. We needed six more mules to move it, I didn't know she planned to kill me—her and some other buck. I didn't even know that he existed.

"The furs were in the Big Horns. I had an old man guarding them for me. I found him dead, just recently killed, but the furs were untouched and she was acting strange. I couldn't figure out what was going on. That night I was in bed and woke up from some noise. She was arguing with him outside the tent. I understood Sioux well enough. He told her she was supposed to kill me and she said no that he had to.

"Damn, that was strange but she had plans for me, I guess. She wanted to get all them valuable hides that winter so she nursed me back to health. Guess they figured they was going to kill me anyway and went on arguing out loud by the tent. I solved all that by getting up and killing the both of them. I got me a sweet squaw that summer and pocketed my own damn money. That money built this fort."

"You sure had some times back then. I better go tell Julie what I intend to do."

"See you at supper."

"Thanks."

Julie wanted to go with Slocum, but he told her to stay put. He had enough to worry about finding the helpers in the snowy world around them and didn't want her hurt.

She hugged him and then they went to bed. He enjoyed her body and reactions so much, and he sure had awakened a real woman within her. Whew, she kept his lower back aching, but hell, he enjoyed even the reminder of it and all the fun they had in bed.

He rode out on a shaggy mustang he chose as a survivor of what the winter dealt out to such animals. McKee thought the men had gone northeast to look for any stray buffalo. So, well dressed for the cold, Slocum left McKee's small ship in the sea of white. Julie, close to tears, had kissed him good-bye. In an hour, he couldn't look back and see the flagstaff any longer. Moving on, he watched for any sign of smoke or movement. In a few hours he spotted some buffalo pawing in the snow for something to eat. These furry creatures had lived in this harsh environment for a million years. But where were McKee's men?

An hour later he saw the sides that kept things loaded on the carreta sticking out of the snow. One wheel must have been broken because of the odd direction the rig sat. He could see the ends of spears sticking in things buried under the snow. As he drew closer to the disabled vehicle, he saw the long-horn oxen steers had both been slain in their yokes and realized those others humps were the bodies of McKee's men.

While he searched the scene, he discovered that the bodies had been mutilated, and under a drift he found a .50-caliber Sharps rifle and a canvas bag of ammo. The attackers must not have found them because of the snow. Anxious about where the killers had gone, Slocum made several checks of the horizon around him. When he cleaned the snow off the rifle, he discovered it had an empty cartridge in the breech. After ejecting the cartridge, he reloaded the rifle, satisfied he had an excellent weapon should he come under attack.

There was no way he could bury the three bodies or even recover them. Hungry wolves would find them and have a feast. He needed to return and pass on the sad news. The cold north wind swept his face. Who had done this? No doubt Indians, but was it Red Bear or some other band? There was a lot to wonder about. Had McKee's men shot a buffalo or two and were they coming home? No way to tell, but he'd better get back. Rifle in his hand, he headed for the fort. Satisfied the mustang would know the way back, he let him have his head.

The winter sun set too early and he let the mustang push his way under the starlight. Slocum at last realized they were going to make the fort. Dogs barked and McKee came out to greet him. Julie came running through the snow to join him.

He handed McKee the rifle before he dismounted. "Careful, it's loaded. I thought I might need it coming back."

"You found them?"

Slocum nodded. "Indians attacked them. They were scalped and mutilated. The steers were killed, too. They need to be buried but I had no shovel. I'm sorry—they were very loyal men to you, I know."

"Could you tell which tribe?"

"I didn't recognize any of the marks on the spears."

"Son of a bitch. I want them punished. Those men were no threat. All they did was work for me. I feed starving Injuns. Why kill my men?"

"I don't know how to figure out who killed them."

"When I find out who did it, they will be put to death. Hear me?"

"Yes, sir." He watched the old man go back into the store. He looked much older to Slocum—much older.

He and Julie joined him inside the store, and McKee spoke to him. "What can we do?"

"Ask people who might know or have heard about the raid. Some Injun will get drunk and spill his guts."

He agreed and turned to Julie.

"It's been a long day for you. Willow will find us some food." Julie guided him back into the kitchen.

"We will need more meat," Willow said. "I have dried meat but . . ." She wrinkled her nose about that.

"I saw some buffalo. I'll go shoot them."

"How will you get them back?"

"Slide them on the snow. Now is the time to go get them."

"I can go help you," Julie said.

Willow agreed. "I will find another woman who can ride a horse and help you."

"In the morning," he said.

The two of them sat down at the long table and another of the women brought them two plates of food. "I am so glad you went to find them. They were good men and we are all sad they were murdered. But thanks so much for going and doing that."

"What's your name?" he asked.

"Kelly," Julie answered for her. "No one could pronounce her real name."

Both women laughed.

Back in the jacal, they undressed and climbed into bed, both of them so anxious it was like they'd been separated for months. His hard rod stroked her smoothly and she hunched her butt hard to meet him. Soon their minds began to spin, and the feeling of the rising in his nuts told him he was about to explode. He did, and she fell back, satisfied, on the bed underneath him.

Slocum smiled down at her. Her eyes at last opened, and Julie shook her head in disbelief. She made him stay on top of her.

"I just don't want it to end."

He agreed.

At dawn, they set out in the powdery snow, Slocum and the two women. They had gone only a few miles when he saw the buffalo. He used a folding tripod to set the rifle on. Kelly held the horses.

He whispered, "We're not far from the fort. We can get two buffalos here."

Julie nodded. He picked out the biggest one and set the

sights. The rifle boomed and the bull fell down without a cry. Next was a big cow. He dropped her and her death was soundless also. On their horses, he waved a blanket at the others and spooked the rest away. He bled them, while Kelly used a hatchet to open the bull's gut. They would weigh less and be easier to drag if they were gutted, though they tried to save all they could. They had to get as much meat to the fort as possible. Kelly saved the liver. Then the women cut out the entrails, which stank of the sourness of a ruminant. Slocum tied three lariats to the bull's hind legs and next tied them to their saddle horns. They began to drag him to the fort.

The job was not easy and the bull's head bounced up and down once they got him sliding. Their horses dug in on the long grades. They really had to struggle to haul him uphill. In no time the hay-fed horses had to be rested, and then they would set out again. Past noontime, they had him at the fort. The squaws changed saddles to fresh ponies, and two other squaws rode back with Slocum to get the other buffalo. Past the early dark of the winter day, they were cheered by the fort people when the cow arrived. The two hostages were good workers though the shorter one never spoke. They all fell into the task of skinning the second buffalo.

McKee held up a torch for light. "I need to go bury those men."

"We need a sled and I'll go get what's left of them," Slocum said.

"It's a good Christian thing to do," McKee said. "Those men served me well. They were like sons to me." The old man looked tired when he put his hand on Slocum's shoulder and thanked him for volunteering to handle the job. "At least now we have enough meat, thanks to you."

"Those women worked harder than I did. I'm just paying for my board and room."

McKee laughed. "You can stay here free anytime."

"You'll need to replace those men."

"I will. There's lots to do to run a fort. These women of mine would not like to live in town. The only reason an Indian woman lives in town is if she's desperate, and then she becomes a whore for the scum. I'll need to find some more men."

"In the spring, I'll take those white women to Santa Fe for you. Collect the ransom money you paid."

"Good. They're fine here for the time being. The quiet one may have her baby here by then. All the women are excited about that."

Slocum nodded. "A baby may find her voice for her."

McKee smiled and agreed. "It might do that. I had not thought about such a thing, but wouldn't that be nice."

Slocum and Julie rode out with blankets to wrap the bodies in, and each pulled a crude sled to bring them back on. A grim job. He told her he could do it, but she said she was his helper and could stand the bitter task. He chose not to argue about it. When she set her mind to such things, he found her very determined.

Midday, they found the murder site and began the grim task of digging out the frozen remains, which had been further ravaged by wolves. Wrapped in blankets and rope-tied to keep them covered, they put two on his sled and one on her sled. Then as Slocum tasted a sourness behind his tongue that threatened to choke him, they headed for the fort.

Slocum also collected the spears, hoping the squaws might recognize the marks on the shaft. Julie had no idea, but she was a Navajo and knew little about the plains tribes.

"They must have snuck up on those boys to kill them, with so little evidence of a fight."

"Or they carried away their own dead."

She nodded. "Those three were tough men. Maybe they thought the braves were friendly?"

"I guess we'll never know why they were killed. I fear they killed them to weaken the fort's security and then try to take it. McKee has some great stores of gunpowder and whiskey, plus yours."

"That belongs to Wolf. I don't drink firewater. One time he made me drink enough to make me drunk—to show me what happens."

"What did you do?"

She booted her horse to go faster. "I passed out and had bad headache the next day."

"Never again?" he asked, amused at the bad face she made for him.

"Never again."

He laughed. "What will you do if he does not find you by spring?"

"Maybe I will go home to my people."

"I thought they'd shunned you."

"I think I can find a man who needs a woman and become his squaw. What will you do?"

"I'll take those white girls to Santa Fe."

"Then what?"

"I'll probably go north into the mountains."

She nodded.

They rode over the frozen land. The sleds hissed across the snow. The loads were much less to pull than the buffalo carcasses and came much easier, aside from turning over once in a while and requiring Slocum to dismount and right them. Otherwise, the trip was uneventful.

McKee's women had the graves dug for them. And under torchlight with his square reading glasses on his nose, McKee read some Psalms over them. They were buried inside the low adobe fence around the fort.

The women took the spears to the house to examine,

but Slocum heard no comment from them about the tribe or where they might have come from. After some food, he and Julie went to their jacal and banked the fire. He caught and held her tightly to his chest.

"I'm very grateful that we met, Julie. You've been my right hand, and when you leave, I'll be sad."

She looked up and smiled. "You embarrass me. I won't forget you. Indian men seldom or never kiss their wives. I have enjoyed you kissing me like I was a white woman."

"You are," he said, then kissed her.

"You kiss me and I am like coal oil, set on fire by a match, and I am ready to take you to bed."

"So am I."

"You are always ready. Even when it is just over." She pushed him backward on the bed and began to take off her outdoors clothing, laughing as if free of the day's grim task.

What a great little woman. In minutes, they were naked and hugging each other for warmth since the room had cooled without a built-up fire going all day. Their mouths locked in dedication to arouse both of them. Her small fingers found his dick and she pulled hard on it to stiffen the shaft. Satisfied that he was soon going to be hard enough, she guided him in the lips of her vagina, then she raised her small butt to accept him.

In a blinding fury, they soared like flames in a hot fire to fly like great eagles in the madness that took hold of their bodies and minds. Their breathing became rapid and heavy. His hard-driving dick in her tight pulsating pussy fueled their desires to become a raging forest fire, consuming them in a blaze that went on forever.

Soon she was on top of him, riding his dick like a bronco rider with her small breasts shaking like flags in a high wind. Between the hair covering her dark eyes, he caught glimpses of the intensity she had for the last blast. He gripped her narrow hips with his hands, assisting her fiery action.

Then from the depth of his balls, he felt the rise of hot fluids, which he fired like a shotgun into her core. She collapsed on top of him and the muscles inside her made pulsating waves on his tight-fitting erection. Their mixed fluids leaked from her over his scrotum as she sprawled on his chest and tried to recover her breathing.

He raised her chin and smiled at her. "You are some woman, Julie."

"I have seen mares mounted by strong stallions that would get so weak from the breeding they would fall to their knees when the stallions were done and lay sprawled on their sides, groaning deep in their throats. I feel like that right now."

They both laughed.

The next week the weather broke, the snow melted, and a caravan of carretas loaded high with firewood came to the fort. McKee already kept a mountain of split firewood next to the main building—maybe enough for two years—but he welcomed the Mexican men as gratefully as if he were about to run out of fuel.

They asked him about the fresh graves. Obviously they were either relatives or friends of the deceased, for the graves drew some tears and grief from some of the hardest-looking men in the group. Many dropped to their knees, crossed themselves, removed their sombreros, and spoke to their Maker.

Money was in short supply among the Latinos in Texas. But McKee would always buy their firewood since he'd need it at some time, and so they left the western hill country for his fort when they had a good amount to deliver. There must have been thirty teams of oxen and they showed him each load. Two carretas had carried the hay for the oxen. They had about used up the first load. But they knew how to ration it out and how much to take along.

The old man knew how to survive in this land. In summer they brought him hay caravans. But in a land of so little money, McKee was their principal industry. They had a fiesta that evening. They raised hell, ate and drank and danced with the Indian women and their own cooks. The silent one did not dance; she sat in the corner, bowing her head. Her sister was different, and agreed to dance with a few of the men. But Slocum noticed that McKee's women acted like her chaperones and kept an eye on her to make sure no one took her away even briefly.

The next day was warm, too, and the caravan made plans to leave—obviously afraid of the next storm waiting to sweep in. Fifty-degree days lasted only a short while on Cap Rock in the winter, and they had a long trip back home to San Angelo. Four young men agreed to stay behind and work for a year at the fort.

McKee took Slocum aside and asked him to teach them how to shoot and how to care for firearms.

"I'll feel much better when we have some trained fighters here. Then you can take them on a buffalo hunt. I bought a carreta and an oxen team to replace the one we lost."

Slocum agreed and they saw the long train off the next morning. The leader promised the old man another fuel delivery in late spring. McKee thanked them and told them to come back anytime, as the creaking wheels began to roll southeastward.

The four young men were in their late teens and early twenties, and Slocum began teaching them about firearms. Carlos was squat built, Rafe was the youngest, Juan was the biggest and strongest, and Pablo was the slowest. Slocum lined them up with Springfield breech-loaded rifles. They learned gun safety first, then the women made them stuffed dummies for targets and Slocum planted posts to mount them on. He brought them blindfolded to the range when it was all set up. Julie and another squaw turned them around so they were almost dizzy.

He fired his pistol in the air and shouted, "You're being attacked!"

They stripped off the blindfolds and stood there, getting their bearings. Some looked around first to locate the positions of the dummies, but Juan went right for the stacked rifles. He ordered Rafe to open the ammo box while Slocum shot his other pistol in the air. And he was shouting, "They're shooting at you! Hurry! Hurry!"

One by one, they began loading and shooting at the targets.

When Slocum called for them to stop shooting, he said, "Juan, you might have survived. The rest of you were killed. You weren't fast enough, and the enemy rode you down. What did I say to do first?"

"Find the weapons and ammo," Juan said with his rifle standing beside his leg.

"Right. You can't defend a fort with your bare hands. You get your guns first, then figure out whether you have to use them."

"Now what must we do?" Rafe asked.

"Clean the weapons," Carlos said. To Slocum, he said, "I see what you mean. If they come to charge the fort, we must go get our guns right away, before we even look to see how many there are?"

"Right. There's no time to think about it. C'mon, let's go clean our weapons."

Within a few days, the foursome could hit the targets with their rifles. Then at rifle range, Slocum had them shoot with cap and ball pistols at the dummies. No one hit a thing.

"Use a rifle for long-range shooting and pistols like knives in close combat." They agreed, shaking their heads about their failure to even come close to the dummies with their hand weapons.

Winter had swept in hard and then defrosted. They set

out to find a buffalo with the carreta and oxen. They slept in bedrolls. They'd brought along enough wood to keep up a fire to warm by and cook on in the morning. He and Juan took their horses and went looking.

They spotted three buffalos grazing. Juan set up the tripod and loaded the rifle.

"Now be sure you hit him behind the front legs and blow up his heart. Even at this distance a wounded buffalo is always dangerous. Be real steady."

The young man took aim and the rifle exploded so loud the report made Slocum's ears ache. The bull crumbled into a pile downrange. He clapped the youth on his shoulder. "You did great. Now go get the crew."

"Should we shoot another?"

"No, we'll have enough fresh meat for a while and then you can organize another hunt."

Juan smiled at him. "I am learning so much. Thank you."

"You learn quick."

They had another fiesta that evening when they returned. Fried liver and the finest rib steaks. Slocum and Julie watched the excited boys talking about the kill and having to run the other two buffalos off, who didn't even know that one was dead.

In a cold snap with feathery snowflakes on the hard wind, a party of white men came by the fort. They had several pack mules, and in their buffalo coats they looked bathless and tough. Slocum, repairing a saddle with Rafe, watched, and then he left the boy in charge to finish the repairs, went to the back door, and came into the kitchen.

"Who are those men out there?" he asked Willow.

"I don't know. They asked if Wolf Ripley was here."

"Why?"

"He owes them money for whiskey they sold him and say he ran out without paying them for it."

"Send someone to tell Julie to stay out of sight. I want to check on them first. They may know her. No names?"

"One is called King something."

"Tell her that."

"Should we be armed?" Willow asked.

"It might not hurt."

He went to the room next to the store and listened. One loud voice spoke about many things to McKee. *The fucking Comanche. The damn army. The badge-toting U.S. marshals. He had a hard-on for Mexican women.*

McKee simply listened to him without arguing and then sold him some whiskey. The men sounded mad about this Ripley guy running out on them. The loud voice kept asking McKee about him as if he thought he'd trip the old man up and get him to admit the son of a bitch had been there.

In the room's dim light, Slocum checked the loads in his .44 and then holstered it. Better go face these devils, whoever they were. When the door opened, they all went for their gun butts.

"Hold your fire," McKee said loud enough only the deaf couldn't have heard him. "This is my partner, Slocum. Slocum, meet John King and his associates."

"Nice to meet you," Slocum said. "Kind of cold to be up here on Cap Rock, isn't it?"

The bearded faces of the other men nodded in agreement, and the four of them sat down. King, a portly man in a dark oilskin duster, pulled the coat back and exposed an ivory-handled Colt with a steer head carved on it. Nickel plated, too. He pushed his wide-brimmed black hat back on his head.

"Maybe you know where that stinking Wolf Ripley's at?"

"He may be going to sprout daisies come the spring thaw."

"How's that?"

"I found his woman about two months or so back in a

dust storm. I brought her here and she had no idea where he ended up. They'd come under attack and she ran away."

"She's lying to cover for the son of a bitch," King swore.

Slocum shook his head. "She doesn't know where he's at or what happened to him. Am I clear enough?"

"You covering for some red whore?"

"Listen, King, you call her nothing but 'ma'am,' or I'll blow you to kingdom come."

King sniffed out his nose, then reached for his Colt.

That was all it took. Slocum drew and fired at him. King's left hand shot to his ear in the cloud of black-powder smoke and screamed, "You shot me!"

"You want the other one notched?"

"Hell, no! I'm bleeding to death." He looked in disbelief at the blood on his hand.

"You got it straight?"

"Help me, boys, I'm bleeding like a stuck hawg."

"Just keep your hands off your gun butts," Slocum warned.

Three men were instantly around him, trying to stop the bleeding with their kerchiefs, and like the others, they were also coughing, their eyes watering from the smoke in the room. Someone opened the door to let the acrid burning fog outside. Willow came in the room and went directly to the wounded man.

She pulled the others away. "It needs cauterizing. Bring him into the kitchen. I'll heat an iron. Who did this?"

"That guy." Someone pointed to Slocum.

"Then he must've needed it." She took King by the arm and dragged him after her out of the room.

"Everyone settle down," McKee said and handed one of them a small crock jug. "You go around and pour everyone two fingers of that."

Slocum holstered his gun in time to hear King scream back in the kitchen. She must have cauterized it. In a short while, he came back out with his whole ear bandaged and he looked groggy. He sat down in a chair. Several of his men watched Slocum like dogs that wanted to bite him but were afraid to challenge him. They asked King if he was all right.

King gave them a grumpy reply. "Hell no, I ain't all right. The bastard about shot me in the eye."

Slocum shook his head and turned to the bar. "If I'd wanted to, you'd be blind right now."

King didn't answer him. Obvious from what he saw in the smoky mirror behind the bar, King was experiencing great pain. Good, it might take some edge off the bossy bastard. He'd make his next shot solid in him if he bothered Julie. Slocum's anger slowly drained away. Someone closed the door. Most of the gun smoke was out of the room, and the store had chilled down. There were five men with King. Everyone no doubt had a past of being tough and lawless. But like most followers of men such as King, they weren't leaders and waited for his decision on what to do next.

That injured ear would sure be sensitive to the cold, and Slocum doubted he'd try anything in case he couldn't hear well on that side or his balance was off. For the time being, King was disabled enough to fear the man who'd shot him.

McKee came down the bar and offered Slocum a drink, saying in a low voice, "Willow said the boys were ready if you needed backup."

Slocum shook his head. "We'll see. There won't be a problem here for a few days. His ear's going to hurt too bad for at least that long."

"You ever met him before?" McKee asked in a whisper.

"Never seen or heard of him. Where's he from?"

"Damned if I know." Then he raised his voice. "Where you guys come from?"

"Texas."

"Helluva big place."

"I come from Fort Worth. It ain't this damn cold back there."

"You boys seen any polar bears coming out here?"

They laughed.

Their untanned buffalo hide coats gave off a rotten odor of cow dung, and it grew stronger the longer they stayed in the heated store.

"You got any whores up here, McKee?" one of them asked.

"Nope, I'm too far from having steady customers to have any."

"Hell, you could charge ten bucks a pop for one and make yourself rich."

"And wait another month for the likes of you to come back. No need for me to have any." McKee sold the man another quart of whiskey and thanked him.

"I'd give twenty," another outlaw said, squeezing his crotch like he had a problem. "Even for an ugly one."

"How many of you are going to want supper?" McKee asked. "I'll get the women to start cooking it."

"What'cha got?"

"Buffalo, frijoles, hot sauce, and apple pie."

"How much?"

"Two bucks a plate or frijoles for a dollar."

"You buying, King?" one of them asked their boss.

"Yeah."

"Buffalo or beans?"

King waved like he was swatting a fly. "Get 'em buffalo."

McKee said to Slocum, "Go tell Willow to bring five plates of buffalo, beans, biscuits, and apple pie. I'm fine here by myself."

"Okay." Slocum stood up, looked over the five men, then went into the kitchen.

He told Willow what they'd ordered. She scowled and said, "I wish they'd leave. That store stinks now like a cow lot."

He agreed. "I guess McKee's making money. They sure are drinking a lot. Does Julie know they're here?"

Willow nodded. "I'll send you two plates down there for your supper. Our boys are standing by if they get rowdy."

"Good. Then signal me, too."

"I will. Maybe they'll all pass out. Do you think he'll ever hear out of that ear again?"

"He'll be fine in a few days," Slocum reassured her.

"Too bad," she said, shaking her head.

Slocum left the kitchen and walked with the snow crunching underfoot toward their jacal.

"Who is with him?" Julie asked before he even got inside the door.

"I don't know their names. One is missing a tooth in the front."

"That is Jocko. He cut up a whore in San Antonio because he was mad at her for not getting his dick up. He's a rat. I cut him with a butcher knife for feeling me up from behind. Who else?"

"Two guys with long beards and black-colored eyes."

"The Norton brothers. They like to kill Indian women. Slowly. Wolf ran them off for shadowing me. Who else?"

"A cocky blond kid?"

"That is the Rio Kid. He thinks he's a fast gun, but all he ever shot were unarmed men. He's cute and lots of women chase him. A rancher's wife met the Kid in a line shack and her husband caught them fucking. He beat both of them half to death with a big stick, then he dragged her home and chained her to their bed. She later ran off and went to work in a Socorro saloon."

"Nice guys, huh?"

She shook her head. "No, they are trea-cher-ous. That is what Wolf called them. Do they know where he is at?"

"No, they came here to find him."

She frowned. "I wonder if he is even still alive."

"Damned if I know. Now tell me what happened to bust you two up in the first place."

"We had traded with a small band of Comanche." She wrinkled her nose. "Those people are so filthy and stink bad. He made a good sale and they paid him in Mexican gold coins. But he expected treachery. So that night he sent me on east with the three burros—one was mine to ride. My burro got away when I stopped to get off and pee. He ran away in the night like something had bit him. I never knew what did that. So I was stuck with those two loaded ones and kept going. I had gone on ahead of him before this, and he always found me. But it wasn't in a dust storm. He spoke of this place so I figured he'd someday come here."

"What did he have to ride?"

"He had a big blue roan stallion and six big mules."

"Loaded?"

She quickly nodded. "But he doesn't owe them for any whiskey. He is smart with money and even made the Indians pay him. Word must have gotten out that those Comanches paid him with gold coins from a stagecoach robbery." She shook her head. "Those dumb Comanches can't even count. Money is like rocks to them. They may have paid him a fortune for what he gave them in return."

"Yes, but why has he not come here?"

"Maybe he hasn't spent all his money yet?" she suggested. "In El Paso or Santa Fe. He had lots of gold coins the last time I saw him."

"That news disappoints you?"

"He is not as nice as you are. But few men have treated me as good as he did. I know you will ride on one day, and if I find him, maybe he'll want his Navajo squaw back."

One of the other women brought their plates piled high with hot food and reported, "They are all drunk and will sleep on the store's floor tonight. Willow said to tell you."

"Tell her to post a guard. And thanks."

When she left, Julie giggled and shook her head. "I can't believe you shot his ear off."

"Not off. I only nicked him. He needed it. That bastard thinks he scares everyone. He doesn't scare me."

"How will this all end?"

"I expect him to ride on and look for Wolf."

"King's a mean man, you watch him." Her words sounded angry so he knew she had strong feelings against the man. No one there knew him better than she did. He reminded himself to keep her safe.

And to watch out for King.

4

His head wrapped in a scarf, King sat on his horse in the bitter cold daylight, angry that his ear still throbbed. His big horse was exhaling steamy breath and dancing under him. He, his men, and the pack animals had left Fort Contention, hard-eyed and grumbling. But both McKee and Slocum were pleased to see them ride on.

Willow, too, looked much happier after they'd ridden off. Even the new men agreed that they were glad this gang had left their place.

Slocum came to the store to drink coffee with McKee, who laced his own cup with whiskey.

McKee laughed. "I loved it. Bang and you notched his ear."

"He's lucky I didn't put his eye out."

"King has a long memory."

"He's got a notched ear, too."

"I'm more interested in who killed my men."

"I have little to go on. Why kill three hunters unless you want to weaken the fort's defense? Those men had no riches. Their other guns were cap and ball pistols they wore as sidearms. They didn't find the .50-caliber Sharps and shells. Why kill them? All I can think of is to make you defenseless, but they never came to test their theory."

"There's lots of mean bastards out here in this vast land. I guess I'll never know." McKee finished his whiskey-laced coffee. Willow called to them, "Your lunch is ready."

"We're coming."

Julie had been helping in the kitchen but she joined Slocum at the long table. "Is there any news?"

"The telegraph is down."

"Huh?"

He hugged her shoulder and laughed. "There's no wire here. A traveler has to come by before we know anything. I haven't seen any besides King and his stinking crew."

One of the Indian women brought a plate of hot corn bread and Kelly came by, filling their bowls with thick soup.

"We love your wife," Kelly said to Slocum. "She's a hard worker."

"She's not my wife, but I agree with you. She works hard."

Willow stopped clearing away dishes. "The dogs are barking."

McKee scraped his chair legs on the floor to get up. The leader of the workers, Juan, also stood up.

The old man told him to stay and eat. He could handle the new arrivals. Slocum decided to back McKee up and excused himself to go out and see who had come there.

The colonel was already outside.

He heard someone say he was there for his Indian wife and his whiskey . . .

Her man was there—Wolf Ripley had arrived. Slocum went through the store, and once outside, he saw the bearded man on a gray horse, with three half-breeds on horses and some heavily loaded mules. Medium built, with too long black hair, he wore ragged clothes that hung on his thin frame. His long-tail black wool coat was soiled and unbuttoned. He sat his too thin gray horse like he owned Cap Rock.

"He's here for his whiskey and his woman," McKee said privately to Slocum.

"That's up to her," Slocum said.

"Who are you?" Wolf demanded.

"The man who found her and brought her here. Where the hell were you at that time?"

"She's my woman."

"She's only going to leave with you if she wishes to go."

Wolf shook his Winchester threateningly at Slocum. "She's my woman."

"You shake that damn gun at me one more time and you won't need her." Slocum said it tough enough that Wolf laid the rifle across the saddle fork.

"I want my whiskey, too," Wolf said.

"That isn't yours," McKee said. "She brought it here. She'll tell us what to do with it."

"Where is she?" He stood in the stirrups and looked around for her. "I want to talk to her."

"She'll be here. But if you threaten her to go with you, I'll feed your dead carcass to the wolves." Slocum meant it.

"I'm asking again, who are you anyway?"

"I am a man concerned about her welfare."

"I told you—she's my woman."

"People don't own people. Lincoln set them all free, and that includes Indian women."

"Who's Lincoln?"

"Before they shot him, he was the U.S. president. But the law stands and I'm ready to enforce it."

Wolf dismounted and ran over to face him. Slocum stuck his .44 in the man's gut before he could blink. "You're getting on my nerves," Slocum said. "You better forget about taking me on, 'cause I'll damn sure kill you. I notched your friend King's ear a few days ago."

Wolf's eyes flew wide open in shock. "King? King was here?"

"He was looking for you. Said you owed him lots of money for whiskey you took from him."

"He's a liar. I never took any whiskey from him. Where did he go?"

Slocum shook his head. "He said he was looking for you."

"He finds me, I'll kill him."

"I'm going to go talk to Julie and see if she wants to meet you."

"She will." Wolf acted confident.

"She might, she might not. That's up to her." Slocum turned on his heel and went back to find her. She met him in the kitchen.

"He's here?" Julie asked, shaking her head.

"Yes, but I told him it was your decision if you went back to him."

She squinted at him. "I must decide?"

"He says he wants to talk to you. I told him you would decide, not him."

"I may cry. I want to stay with you, but I know I have a place in his camp."

She impulsively hugged him. With her face buried in his lower chest, she nodded. "I will talk to him."

"Make him buy a damn horse for you to ride. Don't take a burro this time."

Her eyes wet with tears, she looked up and agreed with him. "I will need a horse. And I will not forget you."

He squeezed her and kissed her. Then released her. She nodded and went to the store. He walked back to the kitchen. The loss of her would be a blow, but he realized she had her own life to live. He couldn't settle down and support her when there was still a wanted poster with his name on it and he was off keeping out of sight of some bounty hunter.

John Slocum had been a captain in the Confederate Army, and when the war was over, he expected to come home to his family estate, marry, and pick up the pieces of his life.

Then he'd been gut-shot by Bloody Bill Anderson for protesting William Quantrill's raid on Lawrence, Kansas, and murdering every man and boy over the age of eight. Quantrill had been on a mission of revenge for slaughtered prisoners of war, including his own brother, but that hadn't been an excuse for killing children. Slocum had complained and been left for dead with a bullet lodged in his belly.

Somehow he'd survived and even outlasted Quantrill's Raiders. By the time he healed, Quantrill was dead and Anderson had vanished. He returned to his family estate, Slocum's Stand, in Georgia, to find that his parents were dead and his brother, Robert, had been killed during Pickett's Charge. He also found a carpetbagger judge who'd taken a liking to the farm. The crooked judge tried to seize possession of it by slapping Slocum with a phony unpaid tax lien.

The greedy judge stayed on the farm—permanently, in a grave, along with his hired gunman. After Slocum's bullets stopped the both of them, he rode away from his family farm and never looked back. But the wanted posters for killing that judge kept dogging his steps, and he had to keep moving, to stay ahead of the law. He could never settle down, not even with a fine woman like Julie.

"Will she go with him?" Willow asked Slocum, delivering a cup of steaming hot coffee to him.

"I imagine so. I told her I'd have to move on soon and didn't know where or when. She needs to be in a protected ring. Wolf offers her some security, as much as she'd get in a group of her own people."

"They shunned her, didn't they?"

"One band did. There are others. But she's a long ways away from them."

Willow standing straight up stood near six foot tall. Although her hair was laced in gray, she was still proud strong and what McKee needed to head his women. Slocum could tell she didn't trust Wolf or his kind as any source of security. But a woman like Julie had to attach herself to someone or a group, and hope they were the lesser of two evils.

"When will you leave?" Willow asked.

"When I have to." He smiled at her.

She nodded that she understood.

He went out back and checked on his horse and packhorse. They were in good shape for wintertime. The hay the Mexicans brought McKee had strength in it. Willow's words echoed in his ear. *When will you leave?*

There was no way to learn the killer's identity. The Indian women could make no sense of the markings on the spears he'd recovered. They didn't even seem Indian. Slocum might as well leave soon.

As he was returning to his jacal, Elania, the former hostage, approached him. Wrapped in a blanket despite the midday's relative warmth, the girl asked, "Is your woman going off with him—that sorry whiskey trader?"

"That's her decision, not mine."

"You're a good man," she said, wrapping the blanket more tightly around her, as if it were armor.

"Will your sister ever talk again?" Slocum asked gently.

The girl bit her lip. "What will she say? That those Indians raped us? That they dragged us around naked to show us off for all the sins the white men did to them and their women? That we experienced the tribal women's wrath, who beat us for being white and who tried to change that by turning us black and blue? That men violated and hurt us to show their power over us? No, it is better that she remain silent. No one wants to hear her story."

"I do," he said with genuine kindness. "When she's able to talk. And I'm ready to listen to you, too."

"Thank you. But now I must get back to work," she said, fighting tears. "They are very nice to us here. However, I hope we can go back to Santa Fe in the spring."

"Yes, I understand."

"No, no one understands. We were raised as a rich businessman's daughters. Protected. We had servants in our house. We didn't know what whores were. We went to church in a carriage and had chaperones. And then we were thrown into the fires of hell. I had never seen a man's private parts in my life. Now I have seen way too many."

"Come spring, you will be home."

"I will cherish that reunion. But after all the hell and torture, I am certain we will be placed in a convent for our own safety, when my father learns of our unspeakable shame."

"Hopefully he will understand. I'll talk to him if you like."

He turned and hooked his arms over the crooked top rail. There was more to this woman than he'd suspected. But she'd had her say and turned to walk toward the back door. No words he could say would give her peace. She'd have to find that herself.

A short while later, McKee's half-breeds, under Willow's supervision, removed Wolf's whiskey from the storeroom. Julie would soon get her things and go unless Wolf stayed around to show her off to Slocum. That he possessed her now. And if he did it long enough, Slocum might simply shoot the worthless bastard and feed him to the wolves. He thought Wolf was smarter than that, however. He knew how to survive.

Wolf and Julie made camp a few hundred yards from the fort. They'd bought firewood from Willow and made a cooking fire. She had taken her things, too, so Slocum knew she was going away.

His Colt handy, he blew out the light in his jacal and barred the door. Someone rapped on it an hour later. He rose. And asked who was there with his gun in hand.

"Elania. I am alone."

He raised the bar, and with his gun ready, he opened the door. Careful-like, he checked around for anyone following her. She was alone, still under a blanket. and she slipped inside. His breath made clouds of vapor before he closed the door. Then returning the gun to the holster in the light of the fireplace, he rebanked the fire with more wood.

"Come get warm," he said.

She came over and held out her hands. "Buffalo chips will never warm you like oak does, will it?"

"No, but it beats no heat at all."

"I know, but this is much better." In a few minutes she was taking in the radiant heat. The blanket slipped just an inch off her shoulder, but she quickly pulled it up again. It had been enough time for Slocum to see that underneath she wore a ragged, faded yellow dress. Moccasins clad her feet, and she watched that her covering did not get too close to the flames and catch on fire.

"I could stay here all night," she sighed, then, realizing what she'd just said, stuttered, "Oh—I—I mean—"

"Stay here as long as you like. I'm not going to hurt you."

"You're so kind," she said, and almost smiled. "I'd forgotten that there are still kind people in the world. When can we go to Santa Fe?"

"Probably after your sister has her baby, if we get a break in the weather."

"How long a break?"

"It will take more time with a baby along, oh, five or six days. But we may need to rest a few days, too, along the way."

"My father will reward you. He is a very rich man."

"I know of him." His knowledge was that the family store was very large and a main trading company.

"Have you ever been married?" she blurted out, surprising herself with her own question.

"No, I could never stay in one place that long."

"What a shame. Someday, when all this is behind me, I'd like to find a nice man like you."

"There are—" He didn't want to reveal too much to a relative stranger. "Because of my past, there are men who would make staying in one place deadly for me."

"My father is a very powerful man."

He walked toward the bed in the corner of the room and shook his head. "Not that powerful." Then he stopped. "Why don't you take the bed? I'll sleep by the fire."

"On the floor?"

"I've slept under much worse conditions."

"You're a good man, John Slocum," she said, then walked slowly to the bed and lay down. For several moments, she remained huddled up in the blanket, as if fearing an attack, but then she relaxed and her breathing became even.

Just before dawn, Slocum awoke and went out to relieve his bladder. He could see a light on in the small kitchen window. The women were up and fixing food. When Elania woke up, he'd better send her over to join them.

When he went back inside, she was already up and preparing to leave. "I should go help them."

"Go right ahead."

"Could I perhaps . . . come back tonight?" she asked shyly.

"Of course," he said.

"I feel safe here. Thank you."

"I'm glad. You're safe with me."

"And I will find a way to bathe today. I must smell like an old chamber pot."

He nodded his approval about the bath, and she ran off. After she'd gone, he fed the fire some more wood. What was Julie doing, besides freezing her small backside off in Wolf's camp? He couldn't help being concerned about the gentle Navajo woman who had touched him. But the poor girl had made her own bed and now must lie in it.

He joined the others in the kitchen. In the candlelight,

he sipped fresh coffee while the women all worked. The fort men came in yawning and stretching. They talked softly about the day's work needs. Feeding stock, butchering a large fat hog and rendering his lard. The women were about out of lard to cook with.

They served the men some fresh-made flour tortillas wrapped around slow-cooked spicy buffalo roast, mixed with mashed frijoles and hot peppers. Elania washed dishes and acted like Slocum was not there. Perhaps she was still afraid of all men, including him.

The day, while cold with an inch or so of dry snow on the ground, promised to be a calm one, not too wrought by a sharp wind. Slocum told Willow he was going to scout some to look for the killer and for her to tell the colonel where he'd gone.

McKee must have been sleeping in; he wasn't up yet. Willow suggested that Slocum take one of the men with him for his safety even though all he planned to do was look for signs. The tall woman sounded concerned. She told him to be careful and for him to be armed with the Sharps he had recovered. He rode northeast in the vast open snow-drifted country that topped Cap Rock.

Twice he saw the travois tracks and barefoot hooves of some small band of Indians. No telling the number of small bunches of renegades avoiding reservation life without many resources and only some cheap black-powder rifles. Trying to live as their fathers had in the once-strong horse-centered, buffalo-hunting societies. A dream that was fast evaporating everywhere in the West.

This was how those red men wanted to live—the way their ancestors had before. But the endless supply of the bison that fueled their past existence was nearly gone.

By midday, Slocum could smell smoke from a buffalo dung fire. There was a certain flavor he recognized that was not from oak like their wood fires at the fort. He reined his big horse up and tried to see the source. Nothing in sight. He crossed another rise and discovered two filthy tepees. Some starving horses stood around hip shot.

Rather than simply ride in and get himself shot, he reined up, pushed his coat back so he could reach his handgun. "Hello the tepees."

A fat squaw ducked her head under the tepee flap and came out wrapped in a blanket. In some guttural Indian language she spoke to whoever was behind her.

"I am peaceful."

She looked at him like she doubted him or didn't understand.

"Where is your man?"

She shook her head. It was a no-savvy kind of reply.

"Hunting." She made a sweep to the northeast.

"How many men are here?"

Another woman, who was suckling a baby, came out of the other tepee. "She speaks no English. We have little food. Our men are hunting."

"The colonel will feed you. Follow my tracks." He pointed to his back trail. "Who killed the fort hunters?"

She shook her head. "No kill hunters."

"No. Do you know the killers?"

"No." She shook her head.

"When your men return, tell them to go to the fort on my tracks."

She agreed and watched him ride off. He never saw the Indian hunters as he made a wide circle before he returned to the fort. When he got back, Juan came out and took his horse.

"You see any killers?" Juan asked.

Slocum shook his head. "Did a few starving Indians come by?"

Juan nodded. "The colonel sent them back with food and told them to come to the fort. You think they killed his hunters?"

"The woman that spoke English said no."

"That the truth?"

Slocum shrugged. "Who knows?"

Juan agreed. Then he asked, "Why are they out here?"

"They know there are a few buffalos left. They don't want to be on reservations and opted to find enough meat to remain free."

"I see. They have a grim future," Juan said to Slocum.

"With their old-style life, yes. But they could join us. Thanks for putting up my horse." He went to the kitchen, and when he stepped inside, he hung his heavy coat on the peg, then his hat. When he turned around, Elania held up a fried pie for him to eat and had a steaming mug of coffee in her other hand.

"How was your day?" he asked her, chewing on the sweet apple filling.

"Cold and useless. Some Indians came here."

"Yes, they were starving. Did you recognize any of them?"

"One I saw when I was a captive. He blinked a few times when he saw me here. I guess he thought I'd report him."

"Did he ever rape you?"

She quickly shook her head then lowered her voice. "I know every one of those bastards that did that to me. I won't forget them."

"Could you tell their tribe? All I saw was the two women."

Her eyebrows formed a frown. "What did they look like?"

"One was short and fat. She acted like she couldn't speak any English. The other one was tall and thin. She was nursing a baby. She spoke decent English."

"Her name is Penny. The fat one is Blue Flower."

"How do you know them?"

"They're Cheyennes."

"You were in a camp with them?"

"Yes. We were traded four or five times when we were out there. Each time, we'd get raped all over again, to see, I guess, if we were still any good. In most cases I could have told them, 'I'm as good as those women you manhandle in your tepees.'"

He put his hand briefly on her shoulder as a gesture of comfort. She flinched, but didn't move away.

"My place is warm. You want to go rest? I swear you'll be safe."

"Sure, I'd like that. I always feel safe with you."

He waved at Willow, who was working behind the counter, chopping up some cooked meat. "Elania needs a break, okay?" he said.

Willow nodded, and he and Elania got up to leave.

"Did you learn anything today?" McKee asked as they went by him. He was seated at a table by himself, dealing out a game of solitaire.

"It was cold as a witch's tit and nothing much out there alive. You spoke to the Cheyennes from the camp who are starving?"

"I told them to come back with their women. You think they're any danger to us?"

"What do you think, Elania?" To McKee, he said, "She knew them."

She shook her head. "No, they're just trying to survive."

"I didn't know there were many Cheyennes this far south and west."

"They're anti-reservation ones," Slocum pointed out.

"I guess. But it's tough with the buffalo numbers so small these days to do that."

"They can't eat cows either."

"No. The ranchers would get mad. Thanks for looking around for me."

"No problem. I'll be taking a siesta if you need me."

"Sleep tight." The old man reached over to place a card in the sequence.

"Thanks. I haven't seen any threat to the fort but they still may be coming. Nor do I know who killed your men."

McKee nodded and went back to studying his cards again. "Well, do your best to find out."

Slocum agreed, and they headed for the kitchen.

He spoke to Willow to be cordial while he put on his coat, hat, and gloves. Elania put on the old but warm coat that Willow had given her. They left the chattering Indian women working in the kitchen. As they walked to his jacal, the young men were loading firewood on a carreta to haul to the main building in case it snowed again and to train the young oxen team.

They waved to Slocum and Elania. Obviously they had seen her leave his hut earlier that morning, but they made no lewd or suggestive remarks. They were all aware of what she'd suffered and knew that, at the moment, she needed an honorable protector.

The jacal was thick walled, with only small windows, so the fireplace had kept it warm and cozy.

As soon as they entered, Elania immediately sat down near the fire, still huddled in her massive coat.

"Are any of the women angry that you left? Or jealous?" Slocum asked casually.

She hugged her knees. "No, I don't think so. Willow will whip you with a quirt if you try anything."

"That a fact?" He imagined the tall, powerful woman using a horse quirt on someone for misbehaving. No doubt she would do that if anyone took advantage of Elania or her sister.

"She laid down the law the day we came. We'd lived like slaves in the various camps, and she wanted us to know that this place would be different."

"You are a brave, strong woman," Slocum said. "Some man in Santa Fe will be lucky to have you."

"I hope I can find one as good as you are."

"You'll find him. He's out there."

"But I fear my father, when we return, will put us both in a nunnery. He'll say we're ruined."

"The man who falls in love with you won't care about your past."

"Do you think so? It's not as if we had a choice." She shook all over in a sudden fury, as if she were reliving a part of that past. "You know Katrina, my sister, is praying for them to put her in one?"

"Really?"

"She *hates* sex, and now that she is so sick every morning because of the baby, she despises men for being the cause."

"Let's rest some," he suggested. "And then it will be supper time."

She walked over to the bed and stretched out, still huddled in the heavy coat. Slocum hunkered down by the fire. In a moment they both fell asleep.

5

"Slocum, wake up! McKee needs you!" He barely recognized Willow's voice, amid the furious pounding on his door.

"Coming!" he shouted, jumping to his feet.

"What's happening?" Elania asked, sitting up.

"Not sure, but something's wrong." He lifted the bar and cracked the door open. Cold air swept over his face.

"What is it?"

"A wagon train was attacked by renegades and they need help."

"Tell him I'll be right up there."

"Hurry. It sounds bad."

"Thanks, Willow." He watched the tall woman, wrapped in a blanket under the stars, head for the main building. After shutting the door, he grabbed his coat, hat, and gloves.

"What can one man do?" Elania asked.

"I won't be alone."

He buttoned his coat and rushed to the door.

"Stay here with me," she begged. "You'll get yourself

59

bad hurt trying to save a wagon train. You might even get killed."

He was tempted to go over and kiss her good-bye, but he didn't want to frighten her. "He needs help. I'll see what I can do."

"No, please don't go—" Then she burst into tears.

He was almost out the door. "I'll be back," he reassured her. "Now stop crying."

"I can't . . ." she sobbed, her shoulders shaking. Sighing, he went over to her, lifted her chin, and lightly kissed her cheek. Her tears tasted salty.

"Don't worry. I'll be back."

When he walked out the door, the sharp cold hit his face. The frost crunched under his soles and he saw activity. The men were saddling horses at the corral. McKee must have been sending them with him.

When Slocum entered the store, he noticed a man with a freshly bandaged head.

"Herman Duval," McKee introduced the man. "He was bringing us things we ordered. Says he was ten miles east of here and a band of renegades attacked him. He got a small wound on his head that the women had fixed."

"My name's Slocum." He shook the man's hand. "How many attackers?"

"Maybe a dozen—but they've killed two of my men."

"You get any of them?"

"I don't know. I left to get help when my two best were killed."

"You have some stick explosives wrapped and ready?" Slocum asked McKee.

"I'll have Juan get some," the old man said. "Have one of the men carry the Sharps and ammo. You may need it, too."

"Yeah, we might. They Indians or breeds?"

"Breeds, I think," Duval answered.

"What difference does that make?" McKee asked.

"Breeds are meaner and dirtier fighters," Slocum explained.

Juan burst in. "The horses are saddled, *señor*."

"Talk to Slocum. He's my commander in this fight."

"Juan, we'll need blasting sticks tied in three-stick bunches."

"*Sí*, I can get them."

"Wait," Slocum said. "We also need each man well armed and we need the Sharps rifle as well."

Juan nodded. "*Sí, señor*, we will have it, too."

"I guess that's all. Alive or dead, we'll see you later, McKee."

"I'm going, too," Duval said.

"I thought so." Slocum nodded his approval. Despite the man's wound, he looked tough enough to be of some help. The four boys were not veteran soldiers but they would listen to his orders.

"Take care," McKee said to him and stood up. "I'd only get in the way."

"We can handle it," Slocum said.

He saw that Carlos had the Sharps. Good, he'd shot it before. The other two had Winchesters, and Willow gave them cartridges in drawstring bags. Once outside, and ready to mount up, he told them to listen to him. "We can whip any army, but you must do as I say."

They, very sober-like, nodded. Their horses breathing steam and pawing to go, they rode eastward across the snow. He told Duval to lead the way and the man nodded, lashing his horse with long reins. Slocum disapproved of his doing that to the horse, especially since they were facing ten tough miles, but they followed the man and kept up with his pace.

In less than ten miles they could see, against the rising sun, the wagons and hear shots coming from them. Good. Some of Duval's freighters were still alive. Slocum told Carlos to dismount and shoot one or two of the riders who were milling around out of rifle range from the wagons.

That would teach them something.

"What if I hit a horse?" Carlos asked, lining up the rifle on the tripod.

"That's as good as hitting the rider."

Everyone else remained on horseback. Carlos took aim and fired the large-bore gun. The ear-shattering round went for the group. A hit horse reared and fell over backward on his rider. Carlos reloaded and fired again. The second bullet struck a man, and the third round cut down another. He looked at Slocum. "More?"

"No, they're fleeing. Good shooting."

"Damn, Carlos," one of the boys said. "You blew the hell out of them."

The others cheered.

"Watch for them coming back. They didn't run far," Slocum warned, and they rode in to join the wagon train.

A man with a blood-streaked face came out to meet them. "What took you so damn long?"

"We came as quick as we could," Slocum said, irritated by the man's sarcasm.

"How many men are wounded?" Duval asked, dismounting.

"Four or five."

"Duval, you try to patch them up," Slocum instructed him. "You other boys help him. Carlos and Juan, ride with me."

They charged off to try to see where the attackers had gone. They reached an overlook and spotted the handful of riders. Carlos leaped off his horse and Slocum nodded for him to go ahead. Juan set up the tripod. The shorter man took aim and the gun roared. In the wind the black-powder smoke was swept away. He quickly reloaded and took off the second rider.

"That's enough," Slocum said, but too late to stop the

shooting. The third shot downed another horse and he cartwheeled over on his rider.

"You did real good," he shouted then charged off to see the results of the young man's shooting. Bailing off the steep slope, Slocum's mount slid on his heels in places, but hit the bottom and he reined up at the first hit rider.

The man had been shot in the chest and sprawled lifeless. Slocum booted his horse to the next downed man. A definite breed, the man was sitting up, holding his right arm, no doubt his injury from the horse's fall.

"Who are you?"

"Joe Black."

"Who runs this band of outlaws?"

The man's pain made him wince. "I don't know."

"You know. Tell me or we'll leave you here to freeze to death."

"His name is King."

"Did you kill the three buffalo hunters from the fort and make it look like Indians did it?"

Black nodded. "King ordered us to."

"Why?"

"He said that way you would starve."

"So he wants the fort, huh?"

Black shrugged.

"On your feet and get ready to walk back to the wagon train. Any tricks and I'll have you shot."

Black grumbled. Reaching the others, Slocum told Juan to take Black back to the wagon.

Then Slocum went back to the other downed men. The third victim of the Sharps rifle had been mashed to death by the horse's cartwheeling. Slocum removed his pistol and rifle, but cast the rifle aside, seeing that the stock had been broken. In a search of the man's pockets, he found some Mexican pesos, a diamond ring, probably a fake, and a gold pocket watch that was engraved to a Drake Thurman. He wouldn't be needing it.

Where was King? He must have been in some squaw's shelter. There had to be lodges made of buffalo hides and also some water close by. What was he doing for horse feed? Indians left their horses to fend for themselves, and they were useless until springtime grass fattened them.

But King was no Indian. He needed his horses, and he had to have feed for them. Maybe the reason he tried to get the wagon train was for the grain, but why let it get that close to the fort before he tried to take it? No one said that criminals were all that smart. Slocum had no liking for the man, and cared even less now that he knew he was responsible for murdering the hunters.

Slocum found nothing else on any of the bodies. Only the pistol was worth keeping.

Juan marched the prisoner back uphill under orders to shoot him if he even tried anything. Slocum and Carlos rode back to the wagon train to see what they could do. He found the wounded men patched up, though two would probably die, their wounds too serious. The other four had less serious injuries and should make it.

The oxen were gathered and hitched. In a short while the train was on the move. They arrived at the fort about ten o'clock at night. Slocum told McKee it was their friend King whose gang had attacked the train and also killed his hunters. The wounded breed's leg was locked to an iron ball, which he had to carry in his good hand as he moved about. Any decision about what to do with him was put off until the morning.

Around midnight, Slocum, McKee, and Duval were still sitting in the main hall, discussing the day's events.

"I fed that bastard King and that's how he treats me?" McKee slammed his fist on the table.

"Maybe, as shorthanded as we are, we can hire those two Cheyenne bucks to help us?" Slocum said.

"Good idea. They don't have any work."

"You are damn sure a take-charge man," said Duval. "Did you have an officer's rank in the Confederate Army?"

"Yes."

"I saw you in the field giving commands to those Mexican boys. Amazing. Thanks again. You saved my train."

"They're good men. I was glad we could help."

In the kitchen, Elania waited, wrapped up in the same wool blanket she'd used to cover herself since her arrival.

When the men had finally finished their conversation, Slocum came to get her and escort her back to the jacal.

"Thank God you're safe," she said when she saw him. "I was so worried."

"I told you I'd be back," he said as they walked together in the darkness.

6

Morning clouds hid the late-rising sun. Like a gray goose's belly, they flowed over the land. Slocum's eyes still burned from the sun's glare off the snow the day before. At the fort, Duval's men repaired their wagons, and took some bullets out of their oxen before they became infected. "Not bad" was the way Duval described the whole thing at lunch— the two seriously wounded men were still alive. The breed was in chains, and his broken arm was set in a sling.

McKee had his men help Duval unload the wagons of grain and food supplies. Most of them were okay. One case of whiskey had some bullet damage, bottles broken, but it was the cheap brand. They planned to reload the hides and furs the colonel had bought from the Indians and hunters and have Duval take them and sell them for him.

Duval also brought McKee some mail that had made it as far west as some post office in the panhandle on Captain Marcy's Road. Probably Tularosa. They were soiled and wrinkled envelopes by then, and the old man used small reading glasses to read them, holding the paper to the light at times to make out the words.

He looked up once and nodded his head in agreement. "Duval, you remember Ole Scotter Hankins?"

"Sure, he was real hell-raiser."

"Not anymore. His daughter wrote me and said he got killed in a fight near Denver. She's looking for a place to live. She took care of him in his old age and figured he had enough money left for her to live on, but he didn't."

"Damn shame. I recall her. She was a big redhead and could outlast any man in bed," Duval said. "How old is she by now?"

McKee laughed. "He was ninety-two when he died so she's probably seventy."

"That old? Damn it's been years, ain't it? I forget how they pass so quickly."

"She said Sidney Boles died last winter in his sleep."

"Now that ole bastard was a wildcat in a fight."

McKee agreed. "We won't miss him. If I see his face when I pass on, I'll damn sure know I'm in hell."

Slocum excused himself and left the old men to their reminiscing.

"Sure do appreciate you helping me today, Slocum," Duval called out as the younger man left the room.

Willow came by and whispered, "She's upstairs bathing. I think she is getting over what happened to her."

"Good," said Slocum, hoping her own father would get over it and be able to move on.

7

Duval rested at the fort for a few days. During that time, one of his wounded men died. The other got better. They buried the deceased in the cemetery. The service was short and somber. The man had called himself John Smith—God only knew his real name.

The night before the funeral, members of the wagon train had sat around, and Duval talked about what he knew of Smith. "He was in the war," the wagon master said. "Wearing gray. We talked about it once. Some damn rebel major raped and killed his sister, and Smith was looking for him then. Smith knew how to get around and knew a lot about who was what. He disguised himself as some general's aide on a special mission for him. He even had official papers."

"Did he find the major?"

"He did, and he killed the man. Then he set out for the West, 'cause they had a five-hundred-dollar reward on him dead or alive under his real name so he went by John Smith. He told me he didn't think the Yankee government really cared that he'd killed a rebel officer, but he wasn't taking any chances."

"He was probably right," McKee said, and they all agreed.

"He never spoke about it when he first joined us," Duval said. "But you know how some men conceal a bad past when they're sober, then open up when they're drunk? He must've worked five years for me, and I never figured how he knew so damn much about military papers and commands, until he got roaring drunk one night and spilled it out. And all the while he'd d been looking for the man who destroyed his sister. Do you reckon he'd been an officer once?"

"I bet so," one of the freighters said. "He could do complicated figures in his head and had more numbers than anyone I know."

Duval agreed. "I always asked him if my inventory had been right after I sold the furs. He'd say, 'Except for one good wolf hide, it's all there. I bet one of our guys traded it to an Injun woman for some ass.'"

The men laughed. Among these outcasts there were other strange men who kept their past a secret. Sometimes the people who traveled west were not just making their way to a new life but running away from an old one.

Slocum spent the rest of the day checking the items in the warehouse. Willow's fresh meat supplies were adequate for a few weeks. The horses were doing great on the new hay. He took the packed snow out of the horses' frogs, then cleaned the Sharps rifle and his pistol until midafternoon when Elania came back from working a shift in the kitchen.

She dropped to her knees beside him on the blanket as he finished reassembling and reloading his handgun. With the gun work completed, he cleaned his hands on a rag, then touched her cheek lightly. She smiled shyly at him.

When she was stronger and more trusting, maybe she'd let him kiss her, or even make love to her—before he took her back to her family in the spring.

Another dusting of snow came that night, reminding him that spring was still a long ways off.

8

Arctic air swept down from Canada, making the already cold days even colder. Buffalo hunts grew more tiring in thick clothes, and anything metal that touched the skin got stuck to it. No sign of King meant no trouble, but when would he come? Sure as hell that bastard would try to take over McKee's kingdom. There was no other reason for him to camp out in the area. There were much better spots on this earth than Cap Rock in the winter.

If only Slocum could find King's camp, then he'd have a chance to capture him and his killers. He awoke at each weak sunrise with the knowledge that he needed to stop the killer with the notched ear. He just didn't know how to do it.

"You're thinking too hard about this," McKee said to him.

Slocum pounded his fist lightly on the table. "There has to be a way to find him."

McKee shook his head. "There isn't an answer to everything. But when it comes, you'll know."

"I want to attack and disable him, not vice versa."

71

"You have a problem, and I can't solve it. I know that you're concerned about our safety, but until you know his location, there's nothing we can do about it."

"That's the hell of it."

"Maybe get drunk. It sometimes solves things for me."

"No thanks, I don't need to hide from it."

"You'll think of a way." McKee lifted his glass and took a sip. "I know you will."

A midwinter thaw came, which everyone hoped would last for a few days. Slocum and Juan saddled up and left with a packhorse to search for King's camp. Elania pleaded with him not to leave her and get killed. In the end, he kissed her on the cheek and promised to return.

He and Juan headed north. Most of the snow was gone except for some isolated drifts. It was midday and they had ridden hard despite the weak sun. The temperature was near freezing though considerably warmer than it had been in the past two weeks.

Suddenly Juan pointed. "Fresh tracks."

The young man was off his horse and brought back some fresh horse turds.

"They from mustangs?" Slocum asked.

"No, see the grain." He showed him one he'd broken open.

"They're headed north."

"You think we're on the right track?"

"Not many people feed horses grain out here."

Juan agreed and they rode on. There were about four riders, or animals anyway. Slocum suspected that two were being ridden and the other two carried packs. How far ahead of them they were, he did not know, but if they weren't going to their camp, he and Juan could perhaps swing around and backtrack them.

Evening came early and they made their own camp. When the sun went down, Slocum used his field glasses to scope for the glow of a fire—something they might not see with the naked eye in the dark. Nothing. They made no fire, slept only a few hours, got up before dawn, and rode at first light. They needed to find water for their animals and this was never easy. Midday they found a frozen lake, and Juan used an ax to open a place in the ice for the horses to drink from.

They rode on and late in the day both men noticed smoke. Slocum told Juan to hobble their horses. Then they crawled out on a rim at sunset and found the camp of either King or some outcasts. Slocum thought their shelters consisted of buffalo robes thrown over willow frames. This made for strong structures with light frames. The willow was lighter to pack than tepee poles.

"What should we do?" Juan whispered.

"We can take those bombs we made and throw them in the smoke holes and blow them up. But we might not live to escape the attack."

"Can we tell which one he's in?"

Slocum used his field glasses. Only a few fat squaws wrapped in blankets ever came outside—to empty piss pots, he figured. The cold had them all stuck inside. But for how long? They had no endless supply of firewood like McKee.

"Where are their animals?" Slocum wondered.

Juan turned up his gloved hands and shook his head. "I have not seen them."

"They have to be here or around here somewhere." Slocum looked west to try to find them with the field glasses. But they obviously were not close by, so they had no plans to attack the fort until spring. That would mean at least six weeks later, after the grass ended its winter dormancy.

Slocum decided there was too much at stake to attack them alone. If Katrina had her baby by the time they got back, in the next warm weather break, it might be time for them to head for New Mexico. Obviously King would be unable to raise a strike force until his horses were recovered, after the grass started growing. That would give Slocum plenty of time to get to New Mexico and ride back.

They turned their horses to go home. If McKee could map out some watering spots, they could grain the horses until they found some ranchers in New Mexico who had feed they could buy. Four days of hard riding and they'd be over the state border, then after a week or more, they'd make it to Santa Fe.

When Slocum returned to Cap Rock, he and McKee had a long talk. The old man thanked him and agreed to the plan—they would keep up their guard but it should be a good time for him to return the girls and collect the reward on them.

Elania was not pleased with this plan, however. She actually liked being at the fort and didn't want to leave. She told Slocum that if her father even mentioned a nunnery, she would run away. "I will not be subjected to that."

"I can't help what he does," Slocum said.

"But Katrina is in no shape to ride that far. The poor girl would lose the baby."

"We won't leave until the baby is born." He wasn't going to argue any more with her. He stayed busy shoeing some horses to be ready to ride or pack on whatever he needed them for.

Still angry, she turned her back to him when she climbed into bed later that evening. Then sometime in the night, Slocum awoke to the sounds of soft crying.

"Elania?" he asked, sitting up. "What's wrong?"

"I'll never find anyone to marry me in Santa Fe," she said, sniffling. "No decent man will want me."

He got up and walked over to the bed. "That's not true. You'll find a good man out there," he said, sitting down.

"Not like you."

"Elania, we've been through this already. You have to look hard to find the right man to marry."

"You tell me that every time. What if I can't find one?"

"Don't give up too quickly. Keep looking."

When Elania raised her eyes, he saw something new in them. No longer fear, but something resembling desire. He bent over and kissed her lightly on the forehead. Immediately he felt a stirring in his crotch.

Damn, he'd better get this girl back to her father—and fast.

9

The baby came five days later. A healthy half-breed boy, and Katrina never cried out or even spoke. The fort women made a big fuss, and hovered around the new baby and his mother. The sun came out two days later. Slocum packed everything he figured they'd need and he took a fifteen-year old boy with him to help. He didn't dare weaken the small force at the fort in case of a raid.

"Will you come back?" McKee asked.

"I plan to, but who knows? If I don't return, I'll find someone to bring Paco back. Thanks for feeding me."

"You're like a brother to me. I enjoy your company and so do my women. They all love you."

"We'll head out early tomorrow. It may take two weeks to get to Santa Fe with the baby."

"I hope the weather lets you get there."

"Proctor will pay for their return. What does he owe you?"

"Five hundred apiece."

"I'll get it and send it to you if I don't come back with it myself."

"If you need some of it, use it."

"I'll try to keep it together for you."

"May God be with you, *amigo*."

The four of them rode off in the predawn the next day, with four pack animals to carry food and supplies they might need, especially if struck by a snowstorm. Alone out there, anything could happen to the weather during the winter. The women had fashioned a baby carrier for Katrina, so she could tie her infant son tightly to her back, like a papoose.

Paco, the youth, was a smart hard worker selected by McKee's women, who said he would be the best one to go with Slocum. His excitement over being chosen as Slocum's helper was hard for him to contain, but on the way he proved he was not only polite, but a real helper at camping setups and loading up the next morning. He asked countless questions until he fully understood something, but Slocum didn't mind.

The cold barren country spread out in front of them, and the open azure sky took up over half of the horizon. They rode on, trotting a lot. Then a site appeared on ahead with a black windmill, corrals, and some adobe buildings. No signs of life but the prospect there might be water encouraged them to move forward as the arms of the cold wind swept over the bundled travelers.

The wind vane on the mill had been turned so the blades wouldn't spin off in a storm.

Slocum dismounted, handed his reins to Paco, and climbed the structure. He undid the vane. The wind made the fan spin and the gears contacted. Next the pump began to work. Everyone carefully watched the up and down strokes of the mill. Nothing came, then the pump shuddered a little, and after a few more spins a trickle of water came out of the spout. Then more and more in spurts until the windmill's efforts flushed the muddy water out of the upper pipe and clear water came out in a steady stream into the dry tank.

Elania shouted. Paco added his voice to her cheer, and Slocum nodded in approval at the production coming forth. Creaky-sounding gears and the splash of water warmed him as he watched the power of the wind draw water from under the ground. There would be water for their mounts and themselves, and there could even be enough for baths at the rate it was pumping.

"Paco, go see if we can heat one of those jacals. If you can, start on that project."

"*Sí*, I will do that."

Slocum motioned to Katrina, who was huddling over her baby bundle. Despite the wind, she followed the youth, carrying her papoose in her arms. Elania took the pack animals after them.

Slocum unsaddled their mounts and turned them into the solid corral. The horses soon rolled in the dust and then went to drink from the tank that the water had begun to fill. There was some old hay in the bunkers to feed them. He still had grain for them though he rationed that. After he'd finished with them, he set out for the adobe where the packhorses were hitched at the rack and did the same with them.

When he entered the dwelling, he saw Paco on his knees holding his hands out to the started fire. He jumped to his feet.

"I am ready to unload," the boy said as if caught sleeping on the job.

"Don't blame him," Elania said, gathering her skirt to stand. "We are all so pleased to be out of that wind at last."

"I know," Slocum said. "This place feels like the Garden of Eden. Open and close the door for me. I'll bring in the panniers."

"Who owns this place?" Elania asked, walking with him to the door.

"I have no idea. But we'll thank him if we ever meet him." Then he laughed.

"Yes, we will."

Paco soon joined him. "Finding this, we were lucky, right?"

"Yes, this is out on the fringe of where I expected to find a real ranch."

"Are we safe here?"

"We're never entirely safe. We don't know all of the threats. So we must be on our guard."

Paco nodded and busied himself stripping off the diamond hitch from one of the packhorses. In a short while they were unloaded and put in the corral with the others. The youth then took canvas buckets and began to haul water to heat in a great iron kettle they'd found. Elania cooked them a meal and the baby cried, although nothing was wrong with him. He simply needed to be rocked, which his mother soon did, and things now felt more homelike in the solid adobe structure.

There was a good supply of firewood on hand but no sign of who owned or used this place and why. No need to worry. They had a place to recover for a few days before they had to set out again. To be out of the wailing wind would help refresh them, and Slocum had to admit that would help him, too. The hypnotic effects of that force made people give up on the hope of ever escaping its hold on them.

He made a check of the area. No fresh tracks or manure told him no one had been there recently. A good sign—and if it stayed that way, it would be even better. Back inside, he stripped off his coat and took a bowl of soup that had been prepared.

He and Elania shared small smiles. No doubt she was imagining what life could be like as a married woman in her own home.

He and Paco turned their backs when the women took their baths. The smell of soap filled the small dwelling and added to its pleasant warmth. The women and baby were at last clean and dried. Paco took his dip and then so did Slocum. He shaved and felt refreshed when he re-dressed.

At sundown, he went outside and checked the weather signs. He saw a storm coming in from the west.

Thank God they'd found shelter just in time, he thought as he went back inside to join the others.

10

Sometime in the night, Slocum got up to piss. As he stood outside, wet snowflakes melted on his cheeks. Was this the start of a blizzard or a simple late-season snowfall? No telling, but he hoped it wouldn't last long.

They stayed at the ranch for more two days as the winds howled and the snow piled up. Then the sun came out, the snow began to melt, and they rode west. The melting snow provided water for them and made the trip much easier. They reached the Mission of the Saints on the California Road, and the muscles in Slocum's back eased some.

After an extra day's rest at the small mission, they headed west again. There were more villages to stop over in as they crossed the eastern part of the New Mexico territory. Other travelers were on the road, and word got around that the Proctor girls were coming home. As a result, they were met in many of the villages along the way and honored by people on the boardwalks, who lined up to see them.

They were two days outside Santa Fe when a group of men rode into their camp.

"Father," Elania whispered, then looked at her sister.

As the men dismounted, Slocum stood up to greet them.

"So you are the man who is bringing my daughters to me," said the portly man who was clearly in charge.

"Yes, sir. My name is John Slocum. Colonel McKee asked me to escort them here and collect the ransom he paid for their return."

"How much?" he demanded, not smiling.

Slocum was taken aback. "I hoped you'd be so excited that your daughters are safe, that you'd come to me with a more friendly disposition, sir. Your attitude is pretty brusque for a man who fathered such fine ladies."

"Ladies? Ha! Listen to me. They have shamed me enough. Obvious they fucked every damn Indian who had them. One bitch has a bastard half-breed to show off their whoring like—"

"Get out of my camp. Before I silence your mouth with a bullet." Slocum moved at the man with his fist on his gun butt. "Leave right now. The people of Santa Fe will be more forgiving than a blowhard like you."

"The people of Santa Fe will laugh at you for dragging the likes of them back home."

"Then they can laugh at me. But they will be more generous to your daughters than you are. Get out of my camp and don't come back."

He stood with his hand on his gun as Proctor gathered the others and rode out.

"Damn him!" Elania swore and shook her fist after him as they rode away into the twilight.

Katrina sat on the ground and nursed her boy, rocking him back and forth to comfort him. She never looked away from him or said a word.

"What must we do now?" Elania asked Slocum.

"Go on to Santa Fe. He's not the only man there. The people in town won't put up with his anger and bitterness. There are better people, who will help you and your sister."

"He's powerful and controls many who owe him money. I told you he might react like this, and put us in a convent. We aren't good enough to be his daughters. We have shamed him by being kidnapped and raped by red men."

"Let's go to sleep. In two days, we can be in Santa Fe and explain our case to the people. I believe they will do the right thing."

He turned to Paco. "Are the horses secure?"

"*Sí, señor.*"

"Good, we leave at daybreak. Have us up and ready."

"*Sí, señor.*"

Satisfied that the horses were taken care of, Slocum spread out his bedroll close to Elania's and lay down.

"I warned you," she told him. "To hell with my father. I'll go someplace far away and never see him again."

"You better stay and protect your sister. She'll need your attention, not being able to speak."

Slocum fell into a troubled sleep, and dreamt that someone was beating the hell out of him. They kicked and stomped and punched him. A woman was screaming, but the beating never stopped until he could hear nothing.

Later on, all he could hear was Paco crying. "Don't die on me here, *señor*. I don't know the way back."

Slocum spoke through numb, swollen lips. "I won't die, Paco. What happened?"

"Those same men came and they beat you until I thought you were dead. They took the women and baby and most of the horses, and they galloped away. They tied up Elania, she fought them, but she couldn't get to your gun to shoot them—I could not stop them either. I am sorry, *señor*."

"Where did they take them?"

"I don't know, *señor*."

Slocum's head pounded and he was too dizzy to sit up. His eyes were too swollen to see much of anything. "Do we have supplies?"

"They didn't take them. Just the horses, the two women, and the baby. I tried to fight them, but they knocked me down."

"Did you hear any names?"

The boy shook his head.

"If I draw you a map, can you go find an amigo of mine who would help us?"

"*Sí.*"

"His name is Don Squires. He lives in Santa Fe and has a saddle store on Plaza Street." Then Slocum lost consciousness. When he came around again, he found the boy had covered him with blankets and must have gone to find his friend, Squires. In the starlight near his head, Slocum discovered a small bottle of whiskey. If he had the strength to pull the cork, maybe the liquor would numb his pain. His broken ribs hurt like hell when his elbow brushed against them. He half sat up, bit down on the cork, and opened the bottle, causing some of the whiskey to splash on his chest. The fumes ran up his nose, and he winced at the sting of the alcohol on his cuts. He hoped the boy would find Squires even though he'd be afraid of Santa Fe. No doubt he'd never seen the likes of the busy streets and traffic.

Slocum took a swig from the bottle, and the whiskey burned his throat and the cuts inside his mouth. It stung his cut lip, but he downed lots of it because he didn't know where the cork went or how to set the bottle down and not spill any. Besides, he needed lots of painkiller all over. The pounding in his head didn't stop but it got farther away from him. He slumped back to sleep.

When he awoke, a young woman was squatting down beside him. "Who did this?" she asked.

He managed to say, "Proctor's men. I don't know their names."

"What can I do for you?"

"I'm not sure. I'm hurting all over. How did you find me?"

"*Señor* Squires sent me. Paco told me where to find you."

"Where is he—" Then Slocum fainted.

He woke up again later, and she was putting a plaster of something on his face with a small flat board like a tongue stick that a doctor used.

"What are you putting on me?" he managed to say through his swollen lips.

"Medicine." She was again squatting beside him. He could see her thin brown legs clear up to her bare ass—not that it mattered to him at the moment. It was obvious that she wore no underwear. That was common among the poor women. The thin dress material was wash worn and faded.

Some of what she had plastered on him with her medicine had stopped the hurting and felt cool. It was the pounding between his ears that hurt the worst.

"Are you hungry? There is food here. Can I cook something?"

He had no more voice to answer her. All he could do was nod, and then he fainted again. At least when he was unconscious, he escaped the hurting and headache. As soon as he opened his eyes again, she forced some hot tea into his mouth, but it spilled on his chest soaked into his shirt. He couldn't get it past his numb fat lips.

Then she kissed him, which seemed odd, until he realized that she had tea in her mouth and was trickling it into his throat. He thought he might choke but he didn't, and after several of her kisses, he got more and more of the tea down his throat directly from her mouth.

At last out of breath, he rested for a moment. "What is that?" he asked finally.

"Willow tea."

He nodded and closed his eyes. Willow was a painkiller, and after a while, it did help. When he awoke again, she was holding his head in her lap. "Have this," she said, and encouraged him to sip small amounts of bean soup from a spoon.

Had Paco came back? No. If he were there, he'd be asking more questions about what he should do. Slocum had no idea why the boy was not back. But this dedicated young woman had seen Paco in Santa Fe. Slocum hoped the boy was safe.

Only once was the woman not there when he awoke. The next time, she told him she'd been watering his horses and putting them on new grass.

Another time, when he had to pee, she could not get him up so he half rose and she caught the stream in a tin can, matter-of-factly, and then asked him if he had any money.

"Why?"

"So I can go get some laudanum."

He had her take the buckskin pouch from around his neck and remove all the coins from it.

"This will be enough," she said and helped him lie back down. "I will be back in a few hours."

"Take a horse," he said in a creaky voice that he didn't recognize as his own.

She shook her head. "Someone might steal him."

He couldn't argue and slipped away. When he awoke again, she wasn't there and it was dark. His time awake was short. But her willow tea had deadened the pain a lot. He realized he did not know her name.

Why did he not even know her name? She'd simply never told him what it was. Or else she was hiding from someone. What was taking Paco so long? Had something bad happened to him—no way to know. Maybe he forgot the way back? But that could not have happened because the boy was sharper than that. Someone had him detained. Had Proctor caught him? He hoped not.

In the daylight, Slocum awoke and managed to crawl out from his blankets and piss by himself. Then he crawled light-headed back to his blankets, which stank of his sweat. No matter. He collapsed and it must been hours before he awoke again.

The woman sat cross-legged on the ground and nodded when he tried to talk. "Is your name Slocum?"

"Yes."

"Men in Santa Fe are looking for you."

"Hell, they left me here. I'm surprised they didn't come back and finish me off."

She shook her head. "These men don't know where you are. They are not the same men who beat you."

"How do you know this?"

"Paco told me. He did not recognize the men who are now looking for you."

For the first time since the beating, Slocum felt a glimmer of hope. "Paco's alive? Is he all right?"

"Yes. But he is very frightened. He is staying with my family until it is safe to return to you. The ones who seek you are tough men."

"Do you know any of their names?"

"One is called Laredo. He is a gringo. The rest of his gang come from El Paso. We should move somewhere else to be safe."

"No. We can't go anywhere. If Paco ever returns, he won't know where to find me."

"Paco is safe now. Do not worry about him. You must get stronger so you can fight these men."

"The men who beat me up worked for the girls' father. The merchant Harvey Proctor. They took the two women and the baby that I brought back to collect the ransom money my friend spent on them."

"I heard he sent them both away to become nuns. The breed son of one of them was sent to a church orphanage."

She went and got a spoon to medicate him. "I will move you to a better place and your horses, too. I can hire some men to help me. They will cost you a few pesos, but I still have a little left from what you gave me."

Slocum sighed. "You've been so kind to me. What's your name?"

"Consuelo."

Sedated by the powerful painkiller, Slocum was hardly aware of the trip, but he did recall the bumpy ride on a travois to a place where the cottonwood leaves made rustling sounds in the afternoon wind. It was already spring down here. The jacal was small, but the water Consuelo brought him was sweet. He could hear an old windmill creak in the wind, but it was behind the dwelling, and he hardly could make it outside to piss let alone see what was in the back.

How long had he been in her care? Weeks, he guessed, but his strength was slow to come back and he withered quickly even on crutches. She bathed and shaved him, brought new clothes for him to wear, and under a straw sombrero, he took some target practice from a chair she set up for him. Then she lined up old brown whiskey bottles for him to shoot at. Despite his weakness, he could still shoot. Barely did he ever miss one.

Consuelo made another trip to Santa Fe and learned that Paco was now an apprentice to Don Squires, no doubt asking the man far too many questions about what to do next.

No news of the sisters. They were behind walls of some convent, locked away from life. When her son was taken away, Katrina never said a word, but the separation must have knifed through her deeply.

One night Consuelo woke Slocum up then crawled into bed with him. "God can send me to hell for leaving my husband"—she made the sign of the cross—"but I don't care. I decided he was not going to ever beat me again in his drunken fits. When I left him, I had no choice but to become a whore. God will send me to hell for that as well."

"When was this?"

"Two years ago. But I was a poor excuse for a whore, too. Too skinny, too dumb, no breasts. They threw me out of the house where I worked. They owed me money, but said I was such a bad *puta* that I didn't deserve any money for doing it. I was simply afraid the whole time that he would find me there and beat me some more. Are you strong enough to love me?"

"I can try."

"Good. If it hurts, you must stop, and we can try again tomorrow."

"Let me be the judge of that," he said, laughing.

He pulled her to him, and he kissed her with as much as pressure as he could stand. She put her finger on his lips to stop him. Then she sat up and struggled to get the thin dress off over her head, exposing her copper body, with its small breasts and dark nest of pubic hair.

"Now you can have me." She snuggled down beside him and he ran his palms over her breasts and flat belly. His attention pleased her and she showed it. He rose up with some pain and tasted her nipples with his still-numb lips. Under his mouth, she shuddered and tried to scoot closer.

Her breathing increased, and he used his finger to be certain she was slick enough for him. When he rose up higher, the pain was tough, but she slipped underneath him and he straddled her. Unable to resist, she used her small hand to insert him inside her gates. Her entry was full with his erection, but she spread her legs farther apart and raised her knees to help him go deeper. Her look was one of shock, but once he was deep inside her, she smiled at him in pleasure.

His efforts were not without discomfort, but the pleasure ended his long stretch of being without a woman and then being severely wounded. At his temples, the pounding increased as he sought her tight depths. Their excitement fueled his explosion, and they rocketed upward as they both came at once, then gradually fell back to earth, satisfied, beside each other.

"Did I hurt you?" she asked with concern in her tone.

"No, never. You were just perfect."

Tears flooded her face, and she could not speak for a moment. "You are not like my husband," she said finally.

"I sure hope not."

Then she asked, "Are you hungry?"

"No. But I may sleep some."

"Fine."

"Consuelo. When you go for supplies—if there is still some money left . . ."

"Yes?"

"Buy yourself a new dress. You've earned it."

She about bit through her lower lip at his words, then agreed with a nod.

The days dragged on. His recovery was too damn slow, but he knew he couldn't rush it. When he was well, he'd go to Santa Fe and call out Proctor to even the score. He walked farther out in the junipers every day to build his body strength. Soon he was jogging on the trails he used in the desert country south of Santa Fe, satisfied he would, in a short while, be tough enough to begin his quest for justice for the two Proctor sisters. His sexual relationship with Consuelo was growing steamier and more of pleasure than pain. Her own self-esteem was improving—she was no longer that withdrawn woman who considered herself less than a full female because of her worthless husband's complaints about her and her body. She'd developed a whole new self-image, which showed all over her.

One day, when she returned from getting supplies, she was even laughing.

"What's so funny?" Slocum asked from the doorway, hearing her laughter.

"You know the boy that clerks at the general store? The blond one?"

"Yes." Of course, he'd never met him but had heard her stories about him.

"He propositioned me today."

"What did he ask you for?"

"Did I date anyone now that my husband was gone?"

"Did he know that you'd left your husband?"

"No. But he noticed that a man no longer brought me there and ordered me around like I was his private slave."

He hugged her to his chest. "You going out with him?"

"I guess I could. He is a nice young man. You are doing lots of exercise. Are you planning to leave me?"

"Not now. I want to learn something about the men who beat me up. I want them to pay for what they did."

She nodded. "I can go places you can't. I will help you find them."

"No. Too dangerous."

"I am not some dumb Mexican housewife."

"Whoa, I only meant that I don't want you to be in any unsafe places for my sake."

"I am not afraid."

"We'll see what I find out first."

"All right." She took his shirt material in her hands and pulled him toward her. "Help me bring in the things I bought, then you and I can play, okay?"

"Oh, yes."

"I'm glad you aren't tired of my body."

He laughed and went for her things in the buckboard. They spent the afternoon playing in bed and after supper they rode horses into the city. He stabled them at a friend's barn behind his house. They slipped into the street in the darkness and walked several blocks to the square. With care, they came in the back door of a cantina and slipped into a booth where the light was dim.

A barmaid came and she took their order of wine for

her and beer for him. He also asked her to speak to Deveroe.

When she agreed and left, Consuelo asked him who Deveroe was.

"A man who knows everything that happens in Santa Fe."

There were some loud whores in the cantina messing around with some men, who made even more noise. In a short while, a man who was about five-foot-six came and slipped into the seat across from them. He nodded at Consuelo and then stuck his hand out to Slocum.

"What the hell are you doing here?" he asked as the two men shook hands.

"This is Consuelo. She saved my life. I brought the two Proctor girls home after a friend of mine ransomed them from the Indians. Their son-of-a-bitch father was so mad and cheap, he had me beat up then he locked the girls up in a convent. Without Consuelo, I would have died."

Deveroe made a sour face. "Harvey Proctor's a real bastard."

"Do you know which convent the girls were sent to?"

"I can find out."

"Thanks. Those girls have been through hell. The one girl does not even speak, she was in such shock, and she had a half-breed baby, but her father took him away. Who does he think he is anyway?"

"A powerful businessman, who does whatever he wants to do. He sent the girls' mother to an insane asylum, so he can frolic with young women."

"Is she insane?"

"The only crazy thing she ever did was marry her bastard husband. Otherwise, she's as sane as you and me."

"I want the names of his henchmen. And a description of each."

"I can have a list by nightfall. It will be in an envelope

marked 'John Smith' for you at the bar. His head man is José Rivera, who's a back-stabbing prick. He lives in a jacal in Pine Canyon at the head of the road."

"Appreciate it," Slocum said. He could find the place and have a surprise for that bastard. "Does he have guards?"

"Some dogs is all."

"Good. I'll be back for the list. How much will I owe you?"

"Twenty pesos."

"I don't have any money now, but I'll pay you when I get the ransom money from Proctor."

"I trust you," Deveroe said and left.

"He's a tough *hombre*, isn't he?" Consuelo remarked, watching him walk out the door as if still appraising him.

"Yes, and he's a good man to have on our side."

"What can we do about Proctor's honcho?"

"Give him the scare of his life."

"Oh, how do you do that?"

"I'll show you. First we need some medicine that will put his dogs to sleep."

She frowned. "Where do you get that?"

"From a *bruja* I know." He started to get up out of the booth. Some noisy men came in the front door, but he was satisfied it was dark enough in the back of the room that they would not recognize him. He hurried Consuelo out into the alleyway. They paused in the shadows to see if anyone was following them. No one came, so they crossed down the alleys and back ways until they reached a small casa.

He woke up an old lady, who shuffled slowly to the door. Seeing who it was, she made him bend over so she could hug him and pat his back. He told her his needs and she nodded. She came back with a small jar and put it in his hand. "You can pay me later. I know you have no money tonight. A few drops on the red meat and they will sleep for a long time."

On their way again, Consuelo asked him, "How did she know you were broke?"

"She's a real *bruja*."

"I guess so."

A cook in a restaurant, who was on a break and smoking in the alley, sold him some small chunks of raw beef for the ten centavos that Slocum found in his pocket. No doubt the cook did not put the coin in the boss's till.

At the head of the canyon, by starlight, he laced the meat with the liquid the witch had sold him. He made Consuelo stay and went on ahead. Three dogs came charging at him, and he hoped there was enough medicine to knock them out. They stopped, growling at him. He tossed each one a chunk and they snapped them from the air. Then another piece for each of them. He began to wonder how long before the medicine took effect. One dog lay down and started grunting on his side. Then the other two did the same. Soon they were all quiet and sleeping.

Slocum went back and got Consuelo, leading her past the oblivious dogs. Noiselessly, they crept up to the house. Someone was really snoring inside, and he suspected it was the man he wanted. They tiptoed inside the open door, and he motioned for her to stay in the doorway. His six-gun in his hand, he crossed the room and could see by the starlight a big, hairy naked man. A woman was beside him— naked, too. A slender young girl. He waved for Consuelo to come into the room and pointed to the girl. She nodded that she understood.

He took a large pottery vase and smashed it over the man's head, then stuck his gun in the man's face.

"What the hell—" the man screamed.

"Shut up or die."

Consuelo had grabbed the young woman and was holding her arms. The girl was too terrified to resist.

"Get on your belly, and if you yell at me again, I'll do to you what I did to the dogs."

"Who are you?"

"Someone you beat up and left for dead. Remember?"

The man peered into Slocum's face, then said, "Shit."

Slocum bound his hands and feet, then rolled him over. With the gun aimed at his temple, Slocum made Rivera open his mouth. He let a few drops of the medicine spill onto his tongue. "When you wake up, leave town. Get on a fast horse and never come back. If you don't, I'll find you and kill you."

Rivera's eyes closed and his face went blank before he could answer.

To the girl, he said, "Get dressed and get out of here. This is no life for you."

The girl scrambled to obey him.

They left for town as the dawn began to pink up the sky. They went back to sleep all day in a livery stable near the square and got up for supper in the evening. Slocum needed to be certain that Rivera had taken his advice. After sundown, he went back to talk to Deveroe.

"Any news about Rivera today?" Slocum asked him.

Deveroe smiled and shook his head as if amused. "He didn't waste much time getting out. I heard he was going to El Paso and maybe on to Mexico. He said he was attacked by the ghost of a madman in the night who was coming back to kill him."

"Who did Proctor choose to replace him?"

"Rivera's second in command. A dumb man named Sanchez."

"Where is he?"

"I think he is camped over by the Rio Grande and won't travel without many soldiers at his side."

"Gracias, amigo."

"I never thought anyone could scare Rivera that bad." The man chuckled. "He was hysterical when he left. He said the ghost swept in, tied him up, and poisoned him."

"Consuelo and I did it."

"Well, it worked, but the new man is better fortified."

"Okay, but he won't dare venture out much after his tough leader was run off."

Deveroe left, and Consuelo squeezed Slocum's arm. "What next?"

"I want to talk to Proctor's wife. She's a victim of his bullying, too."

"How will you do that?"

"I need a young lawyer."

"Where will you find him?"

"In his law office, I guess. We'll need a rebel. Someone who's willing to take chances."

"They're all closed now."

"Our man may not be."

"Why is that?"

"A brand-new lawyer might have to sleep in his office until he makes enough money to afford a house."

They left the cantina.

They saw a light in a small office off the square. Seeing a young man working at a desk, Slocum knocked. The man rose and came to the door. "How may I help you?"

"There's a woman being wrongly held in an institution by her husband."

"What would you like me to do?"

"Get her released."

"Who is she?"

"The wife of Harvey Proctor."

"He's a big businessman."

"I know but she shouldn't be held in the insane ward. She's not crazy and deserves part of his fortune."

"Who are you?"

"Friends of hers and her daughters. My name is Slocum."

"Where are her daughters?"

"Being held in a convent against their will."

"What?"

"You heard me. The man is an animal."

"Come inside. Tell me all about this situation."

The man opened the door and motioned for Slocum and Consuelo to enter. There was only one's visitor's chair, which the lawyer offered to her. Slocum remained standing as he explained what happened.

"Elania and Katrina Proctor were kidnapped by Indians, who ransomed them to a friend of mine. I brought them here with Katrina's newborn son from West Texas. I asked Proctor to repay the ransom money, but he refused and had his men beat me up. Then he took the girls and sent them to a convent against their will and shipped his newborn grandson to an orphanage. Since then I learned that he'd packed his wife off to an insane asylum. She isn't crazy. He's the one who's mad."

"I can talk to the judge and ask for a hearing."

"How can I help you?" Slocum asked.

"Give me a few names of people I can call on to testify."

"I'll get them and be back in the morning." They left the young man, and Slocum took Consuelo back to talk some more to Deveroe.

"What do you need now?" the man asked, slipping into the booth and looking shifty-eyed at the smoky bar room for anyone peering at them.

"Five tough men to meet me at the stables down the street before dawn. Pays twenty a day, tell them to bring their guns, knives, and horses. Where does this man who works for Proctor live at?"

"A man named Frisco will bring the men. He knows Proctor's setup down there. They'll earn their money."

"Good, I won't bother you much more. I hired a lawyer named . . ." He turned to Consuelo, but she lifted her hands up and shrugged.

"His office is half a block down the street and he has reddish hair."

"Fred Golden. New man, he should be eager. Needs the money."

"He agreed to talk to the judge about freeing Proctor's wife. What's her name, by the way?"

"Camilla. Lovely woman. And he's such a sorry rich bastard."

"What about the new guy in charge?"

"Sanchez? A dumb dickhead."

Slocum chuckled. "You must like him. Tomorrow I need to tell Golden the names of a few people who can help him get Proctor's wife out of the nuthouse."

"I can get a bunch of them."

"You handle it, and find out where Proctor sent those two girls. I promised the elder daughter, Elania, I'd get them out of there if he did that."

"No problem. Can I go play cards for a while?"

"Hell, yeah. Thanks."

Deveroe paused and put his hand on Slocum's shoulder. "Frisco's a tough man. You'll like each other."

When he'd left, Slocum and Consuelo went out the back way into the alley and hid in the shadows. A few minutes later, some guy busted out the back door, looking both ways like he was on their trail. Slocum stuck a gun muzzle in his back. "Lose us?"

"What'cha talking about?"

"You were paid to trail us." He jerked his pistol free and then busted the man over the shoulder with the barrel of it. The man went to his knees, screaming in pain.

"Who paid you to follow us?"

"I ain't saying."

"I can fix the other shoulder next."

"Harvey Proctor."

"You've got fifteen minutes to get out of Santa Fe. By

horse or on foot, I don't care, but if I see you ever again in this town, I'll shoot you between the eyes and say you were wanted in Texas for murder. Now get out of town. One—"

"I'm going. I'm going." The man got up and flew down the alley.

"Guess he won't track us anymore," Consuelo said, amused.

"I'm tired of all these bastards. Tomorrow Proctor won't have an army any longer."

Before dawn, five dark-faced men arrived at the stables, hitched their horses outside, and came into the interior, which smelled strongly of horse piss and sweet hay. They wore large sombreros and noisy spurs that jingled.

"Ah, you are the *hombre* who asked for us?" the tallest man, clearly the leader, said. "You must be Slocum. I am Frisco."

"I'm Slocum. My friend says you know all about this man Sanchez."

"We all know him well. This is my brother Miguel, next comes Fernando, the third man is Baca, and Sonora is on the end."

Slocum nodded to each of them. "Good to have you here."

"One word, *señor*," Miguel said. "We want to know how you scared the piss out of Rivera." He was obviously amused by what happened.

"I fed his dogs a sleeping potion that a *bruja* sold me. While the dogs slept, I busted a large pot over his head, then tied him up and made him open his mouth. I put a few drops of that potion on his tongue and told him, before he passed out, that if I saw him in Sante Fe again, I'd kill him."

Frisco and the others laughed. "He told me a dozen men held him down," Frisco said.

One man added, "He said their leader was a ghost."

Frisco asked, "You want Sanchez killed?"

"I want him and all his men to leave the territory and stay gone. We're taking Proctor to court."

"He's a powerful man. He may own the judges."

"Then let's destroy his army and take away his power. I owe him for the beating I took from them."

"We're ready."

"You lead, Frisco. You know the way," Slocum said.

They mounted and left in a hurry. He and Consuelo were forced to push their horses to keep up. When they were on the country road leading west, Frisco reined up. "We must circle this place from the back. They will expect us to make a frontal attack."

Slocum agreed.

From where the road forked, Frisco sent the four men to go south. He, Slocum, and Consuelo would come down from the north. The plan was to strike them at high noon.

Things went well and they were approaching the ranch from the backside. A shot rang out, and Slocum told Consuelo to stay back. He charged his horse after Frisco's and they went through a peach orchard like they were on fire. Obviously some of Sanchez's had men made it to the adobe house and were firing from the windows.

Frisco's other men were all right and waved to show him where they were at. Dismounting with his rifle in his right hand, Slocum moved in closer. A few more shots came from the house. Slocum took aim at a window where one shooter had popped up to fire at them. When he shot again, Slocum returned fire and silenced his shooting.

The man's screams were loud enough to make the whole crew nod at Slocum's accuracy. Another shooter took his place and it took two shots to silence his shooting. Then someone shouted, "We give up!"

"Come out unarmed," Frisco said.

Seconds ticked by, but then the men filed out with their hands high. Frisco ordered them on their knees. "Any tricks and you all will die."

Guns drawn, they closed in on their captives.

"Sanchez is not here," Frisco whispered to him. "Or he's hiding inside."

Slocum nodded. Not familiar with the man on sight, he asked Frisco what should they do.

"Talk to his men," Frisco said.

"Where's your boss?" Slocum demanded.

"We don't know," a man said. "He rode out early."

"There are two dead inside," one of Frisco's men reported, coming out of the jacal's front door.

"Find a shovel," Frisco said. "These men can bury them. *Ándale!*"

"What should we do with the rest of them?" Slocum asked him quietly away from the others.

"We could shoot them and put them in the same grave."

"The authorities won't like that."

Frisco nodded. "You're right. We can drive them down the river today, and if they come back . . ." He drew the side of his finger across his own throat, like a knife. "They will know to move on. We can find their leader, too. By dark, he will disappear—or join the others who stopped breathing today."

Slocum and Consuelo rode back to town. They were silent most of the way. She finally spoke. "I should hire that Frisco if my husband comes back, eh?"

Slocum laughed. "He's a tough man."

"What will we do for money until you force Proctor to pay you what he owes?"

"McKee trades with a man named Diego who is in business here. He will advance me some money. We'll go see him when we get back to town."

After they ate lunch bought from a vendor, using the few centavos they had left, then found Pedro Diego in an office at the back of his large warehouse. The place echoed despite the stacks of food items, furs, and dry goods in there.

"Ah, Slocum," the short man said after standing and taking off his gold-framed reading glasses. "How are you? And good afternoon, lovely lady."

Consuelo giggled in response.

Slocum explained about the kidnapping, the ransom, and Proctor's reaction to the return of his daughters and grandson.

"That Proctor is a mean man," Diego said angrily. "He has his beautiful wife confined to an insane asylum so he can be free to screw his mistresses. He is not well liked in this city."

"I hired a lawyer to get her out. The daughters, I understand, were sent to a convent."

"I don't doubt it. How much money do you need?"

"Today two hundred. I may need more. McKee will pay you on your next shipment to him."

"Don't worry. McKee is a man of his word. I'd even pay that and more to see Proctor disgraced and run out of town on a rail."

"Agreed. Now how should I get those girls out of the convent without bloodshed?"

"I will talk to the bishop about such a release for you. Messing with the Church can be bad business, but I may be able to persuade him."

"I promised Elania, the elder one, I'd get them out if their father locked them away."

"I understand. Now what about his wife's incarceration?"

"My lawyer, name of Golden, is working on that case. A bright, hardworking young attorney who needs the money."

"Good. My wife will feel better if you get her released. They were friends." Diego wrote something on a piece of paper and handed it to Slocum to sign. "I'll make it three hundred, and if you need more, come back. Anything I can do, just ask."

"This morning we sent Sanchez's men packing. If he shows his face in town, he'll be taken care of."

Diego straightened up from getting the money out of the safe. "I supposed it was you who sent his henchman, Rivera, packing a few days ago?"

"Yeah, that was us—Consuelo and I."

"He ran away like the scalded dog he was. All of Santa Fe owes you a debt for getting that bastard gone."

"Where can I find Proctor?"

"I doubt he is at his business. With Rivera gone and Sanchez missing, I'll bet Proctor is staying well guarded at his casa on the mountain off the Taos Road."

When Slocum looked over at Consuelo, she nodded that she knew the location. He turned back to Diego to have him count the paper money out in his hand and then he put it deep in his pocket.

With a nod, Slocum thanked the man. "I'll be in touch or send Consuelo to tell you what has happened."

Diego smiled. "She is prettier than you are anyway. Good luck. I will see the bishop this afternoon for you about the women."

They left his warehouse and rode back to her place after reading the sign on the attorney's door: BE BACK LATER TODAY.

"Well, all we can do now is wait. Maybe both this lawyer Golden and Diego will help us enough that we can confront Proctor and collect the ransom money. Plus get those two women out of their confinement. It's a big mess."

At Consuelo's place, they unsaddled their horses and put them in the corral. Then she hurried him into the casa.

"Good. Finally I have you to myself. Get undressed, *hombre*. We have some catching up to do."

He kicked his boots off, then shed his pants, shirt, and long johns. The radiant heat from the fireplace warmed his bare skin. He hung his gun belt on the ladder-back chair so it was handy.

Consuelo had already thrown off her clothes and was waiting in the bed, naked, for him. As he approached, she scooted over to make room for him and held up the covers. Her skin felt warm against his as they faced each other and kissed, getting snuggly with each other. Then he fed on her hard teacup breasts under the covers.

With soft moans coming from her mouth, Consuelo writhed in pleasure. Her hips would hardly stay down as his hungry attention feasted on the rock-hard nipples. His hand ran down over her taut stomach muscles and through the pubic nest until she opened for him, to allow for his two-finger entry through the lips of her vagina. Their breathing grew wilder and she was near mad with need when he climbed over her legs and rose up on his knees. He shoved the head of his iron dick into her gates, easy-like at first. With a gasp, she clawed her nails on his back and he thrust deep inside her. They were a perfect fit, and the contractions inside her welcoming warmth proved to be fierce.

Her fervor in having sex sent him spinning out of control. The ropes under the bed squeaked and strained as he plunged in and out. When he came at last, he grasped the cheeks of her ass, pushed all the way to the end of her inner walls, and exploded. Consuelo screamed as she came with him, and together they soared like two eagles, higher and higher to the edge of the sky. And when he'd emptied himself inside her and her pulsing ceased, they floated downward, exhausted, back to earth.

Consuelo closed her eyes as her breathing slowed. They were both drenched in sweat. Slocum smiled down at her, but she was so weak that she only sighed and snuggled up against him.

Holding her against his body, he rocked her and kissed her face. Soon he kissed her lips gently. Finally he raised her chin with the side of his fist. "You're a hell of a woman, Consuelo. Some man in Santa Fe will be lucky to have you."

"Someday perhaps," she murmured, as if drifting off to sleep. "But as long as you are here, I'm yours . . . and you'll all mine."

11

Later in the day, Slocum rode into town, went to the
butcher, and bought some fresh-cut steaks, along with two
bottles of red wine from a nearby store. Most of his pain
from the beating was gone. After he returned to the casa,
dismounted, and handed Consuelo his purchases, she
kissed him and ran inside to start cooking. He put up the
horse in her pen. So far, things were going according to
plan. But getting justice for the Proctor sisters was his next
wish. And if the lawyer could get the judge to release their
mother, things would be even better.

A man with his sombrero in his hands came politely to
Consuelo's door after dark and asked for Slocum.

"What is it?" Slocum asked.

"*Señor* Frisco said to tell you that the one you talked
about today is dead."

Slocum wanted to ask him how but instead thanked
him for the message. "Also tell Frisco thanks for me."

The man nodded and hurried off.

"Sanchez?" Consuelo asked.

"Yes."

"Come eat. The steak is ready and I have some baked yams with brown sugar and cinnamon on them."

"Oh, how nice." He hugged her. All Proctor had left were his house guards. He would clamp down on him soon.

First he needed Golden to get Proctor's wife, Camilla, out of the insane asylum. That might take some time. Courts worked slowly, but maybe with people standing up for her, it might move faster.

Two days later Slocum rode into town for a meeting with Fred Golden. According to the young lawyer, the judge's own wife ordered him to get Camilla released as soon as possible. Slocum told him that the trader Diego was going to talk to the bishop about getting Proctor's daughters released.

"Damn. You have a lot of things going on," Golden said, sounding impressed. "The word is out that someone destroyed Proctor's army."

"They won't bother you if you're concerned."

Golden smiled. "I'm not but it is funny. Proctor may realize that his position is not so secure here much longer. We have a hearing on Friday for his wife's release. There are ten prominent women willing to testify that Camilla is not crazy."

"Have you talked to her personally?"

"Yes. And I ordered a new dress for her to appear in. I also told her that you were heading this campaign and how much you had done for her and the daughters. She's anxious to thank you."

"I'm not so concerned about being thanked as much as I am to have her free. We may need to sue Proctor to get him to support her and his daughters."

"Get ready." Golden smiled. "I want that cheap son of a bitch to squeal like a pig caught under a gate. I think we can make that happen. It would have been cheaper for him to have paid you the ransom in the first place."

"A *lot* cheaper."

Slocum then went to see Diego at his warehouse. When he walked into the man's office, Diego jumped up, looking relieved. "I have been trying to find you for twenty-four hours. You will need a buckboard to go pick up the older girl. Her sister, Katrina, wishes to stay at the convent, but Elania is anxious to leave as soon as you can get there."

"Wonderful. There's no need for a buckboard. She can ride double on my horse. Where is the convent at?"

"Ten miles up the Taos Road. The head of the order knows you will be coming."

"I'll go right away."

"Where will you take her?"

"Maybe she can stay with a man I know."

Slocum left the warehouse and rode to the square. He slipped into Golden's office. The young man looked up.

"Slocum, you're back?"

"Do you have a wife or mistress?"

"No. Why?"

"Elania Proctor will need a place to stay when she leaves the convent. Can I count on you?"

Golden nodded like he understood. "I can learn more about her father's business from her, can't I?"

"Yes, I guess you could."

"I'll be ready for her arrival."

"I should be back by tomorrow."

"Slocum? Thanks for your help."

He left on the run, got his horse, and rode north. The weather was cool, but not cold. He found the convent and dismounted, then knocked on the door.

He waited for someone to answer, was tempted to knock again, but then he waited.

Finally a woman answered the door and said, "Yes, sir?" He'd expected a big broad-shouldered cow of a nun to answer. Instead he was greeted by a short pretty woman carrying a candle holder.

He removed his hat. "I'm John Slocum. I'm here to get Elania Proctor."

"Oh, yes, *Señor* Slocum. I will tell her you are here."

She never invited him inside and closed the great door. No problem. Maybe men were not allowed inside. He didn't know what was proper for such a place. He waited in the starlight and glanced around.

The longer he stood there, the more he wondered if he was alone. His horse acted interested in something and had tried to turn around at the rack where he'd hitched him. He felt for the Colt on his side. He wished they would hurry up. He hadn't noticed anyone following him—but if they knew his destination, they would not need to follow him closely.

Elania soon appeared with a small bundle and dressed in a long wool coat.

"Thank you, sister," Slocum said to the nun who'd delivered her.

"How are we getting back to Santa Fe?" Elania asked him.

"On my horse. But I think we'll have company. I didn't notice anyone behind me, but the horse acts like something is out there." He undid the reins and stepped into the saddle, then reached down for her to catch his arm so he could toss her behind him. "Be ready for a rough ride if we have to make a run for it."

She hugged his waist. "I can't even believe this is happening."

He swung the horse around and headed for the back of the large building. For an instant he thought he heard someone shout. He rounded the back of the large dark structure and headed for the junipers. In an instant, the sounds of angry mounted horsemen came after them, but he and Elania were already deep in the cover.

After stopping his horse, he set her down. Off the horse himself, he took his rifle out of its scabbard and had her hold the horse and quiet him down. Their pursuers had gone past them, but he could still hear them.

"Who are they?" she whispered. "My father's army?"

"No, they are no more. Paid assassins, I suppose. I hired a lawyer in Santa Fe. You may not know it, but your father has your mother in an insane asylum."

"Oh, no." She slapped her hand to her mouth.

"Oh, yes. He did that, too. We need to take the back roads. I'm going to leave you with the lawyer when we get there."

She clutched his arm fearfully.

"He's an honorable young man. He's working to get your mother out and to force your father to support all of you."

"My, you have been busy."

"Did they tell you I was coming?" he asked.

"Yes, but I could not convince my sister to come out. I told her I would adopt her son." She shook her head. "Maybe my mother can go talk to her. But I did not know she was in confinement, too. My father's a cruel, worthless man."

"I agree with you." Proctor was a worthless bastard. Slocum would get him someday. Someday soon.

He knew they could not return to Santa Fe on the main road, so they traveled the back roads and rented a room in a small village late that night to get some sleep. He braced a chair against the door to ensure no one broke in while they rested. Elania curled up on the only bed, and Slocum leaned back in another chair next to the door. They both managed to sleep until well after the sun rose. Before they left, the woman who'd rented them the room fed them some bean burritos. They rode on and, by evening, reached Golden's office, going around to the back.

They knocked on the back door, and the lawyer answered it. He let them inside and Slocum introduced them.

"I'll light a lamp," Golden said.

"Don't. We had a close call up there where I got her last night. Obviously some hired assassins knew I was coming and tried to trap us." He turned to Elania. "Keep the doors locked when he's not here."

"Of course. Will I see you again?" she asked anxiously.

"I can't tell you that. I don't know, but Mr. Golden will care for your needs. I'll be around, but I'll try to not lead anyone here."

"I understand your concern, Miss Proctor," the lawyer said. "But you're quite safe here. I'm working hard to have your mother released. She is very anxious about your safety."

Elania leaned over and kissed Slocum good-bye on the cheek. *"Gracias, mi amigo."*

Slocum left the two young people glancing at each other shyly and hurried out the back door. In the saddle, he headed for Consuelo's casa in juniper country south of Santa Fe. When he arrived there, she ran out to greet him.

"I feared they had caught you again." She stood on her toes to kiss him.

"No." He smiled at her sweet affection. "Elania is safe for now. But hired men tried to capture us when I got her. We managed to escape them in the darkness and came the long way back."

"Good, would you like a bath or lunch first?"

"Bath, huh?"

"Come, I have some hot water to add to the barrel."

"Good. No one has come around?"

"No one. Not even my sorry husband," she assured him, laughing. "What must you do next?"

"Let New Mexican law work. It's the only way to legally get the mother out of the crazy house. But several important wives are involved in getting her released."

He began to undress. "That will decide her fate."

"He will have powerful lawyers."

"Golden is a fighter. His future as a lawyer may depend on if he wins."

"Oh, yes." She was armed with a brush when he stepped into the tub. He smiled. As she brushed his back, he sighed. "This feels good."

"I was concerned," she said. "When you didn't come back, I was afraid you had found a better woman to sleep with."

"There's no problem there. You are a very sweet, terrific woman in bed, and I knew I must come back and sip more of your honey."

"You sure know how to pump me up." She looked embarrassed.

"No." He caught her brush. "You need to have more faith. Any sensible man would love to share your bed."

"Why?"

"Because I said so."

She laughed and threatened to whack him with the brush. He stood up and she grabbed the rinse water and climbed on a chair to pour it over him.

"Whew, that was cold."

She ducked and laughed. Setting down the pail, she said, "Sorry."

Then she started drying him off. "Would you like me to go to bed with you or eat?"

"What do you want me to do?"

She snickered. "Go to bed."

"Then let's do that."

"Whew, I thought you'd never ask me."

Laughing, he swept her up in his arms. "You are some woman."

"You are nice, too. I never expected a man like you to even find me interesting."

"That husband you had was depressing you with all his bad talk. Don't accept another like him."

"Oh, I won't. I am sure now that you are right."

In her bed, they settled down to soft sex and soon she became so excited she could hardly catch her breath. When they'd finished, they slept, connected, for several hours.

He stayed close to Consuelo and her place for the next few days. Finally, he rode into Santa Fe to find out about Mrs. Proctor. First, he went to see Diego. The merchant told him that his wife had been checking on the case and the judge would be granting Mrs. Proctor's release by the end of the week. Slocum thanked him and went to see Golden next.

They went into his back room, so no one could see them from the front windows.

Golden perched himself on the edge of an old wooden table while Slocum sat in the only chair.

"I heard that the judge was going to release Mrs. Proctor in about a week. What about the civil suit for their financial care?"

"We can win that. When we show his actions to get rid of his wife and girls, the court will be hard on him."

"That might make you vulnerable to harm."

"I'll watch closely."

"Send word to Diego if you need help. He worked for you behind the scenes to get Camilla out."

"His wife really did, too."

"I know." Slocum stared hard at the young man. "Are you being good to Elania?"

"Oh, yes, and she is being wonderful to me. I can hardly wait to get back to her."

Slocum nodded. "Good. She may be rich enough soon for you to consider marrying her."

"Yes, but I think I would anyway. I don't care about her past. So thanks. You've really helped me. And I see now that my business is on track to do more business."

"Good luck." Slocum rose to leave, glad that Elania would finally be able to put her ordeal behind her.

He went by the cantina and asked Deveroe if he knew

of the men that Proctor had hired to get him and Elania up at the convent.

"I think they came up from Bernalillo."

"You have any idea who they are?"

"I can find out. You want Frisco in on the deal?"

"If they are still trying to get me, yes."

"I will have all the information I can get on them by the day after tomorrow."

"How many men are at Proctor's mansion?"

"Three or four. Most of them ran off after the big man left him and the rest were done in at the ranchero."

"That means the remaining ones are tough?"

"Yes."

"I will see what I can find out."

"Thanks. Maybe if I can separate him from the rest, it would work."

"He has a mistress he visits often. The place is on San Bella Street. The house has a fence and an iron gate. Pink house in the middle of the block past El Grande Road."

"I can find it. What's her name?"

"Dolores."

"I'll see what I can do about that."

Slocum found a pair of handcuffs, a dusty sombrero, and a faded serape in a secondhand store for fifty cents, and he soon blended in on the streets with his disguise. The house looked very expensive, and he managed to see the dark-eyed Latin beauty watering her flowers behind the fence. She looked expensive, too, and had large tits that swung around inside her dress as she moved. The sight of them amused him.

A fancy carriage delivered Proctor, very late that afternoon, to her front gate and then drove away. No sign of a guard anywhere and he heard Proctor tell the driver to be back for him at midnight. The gate clanged shut and the man hurried to her front door. In the doorway, she came with open arms to greet him, including him in a big hug of her boobs. It was sundown, and Slocum knew that the woman in the kitchen was busy fixing them supper. He regretted that later he would have to handcuff and gag her.

But it was all part of his plan. He waited for her to finish serving the supper and then gathering the dishes. He slipped into the kitchen and put his hand over her mouth. "If I have to knock you unconscious, I will, but be quiet and come into the closet and I won't hurt you."

She obeyed, but he could see that she was really worried he was planning to rape her. He handcuffed her then gagged her and made her sit on the floor. He told her he hated to do that to her but it was necessary. He told her not to worry; he had no designs on her or her boss, Dolores, either. Then he walked quietly upstairs and heard the noisy lovers in a bedroom. With a gun in his hand, he banged on the door.

"Stop screwing your mistress, Proctor, and get out here."

The noises abruptly ceased.

"What the fuck is going on?" a male voice called out.

"Now," Slocum demanded, "or I'll break this door down."

He heard a woman's soft scream then fumbling, bed springs creaking, and heavy footsteps approaching the door before it was flung open.

Wild-eyed and enraged, Proctor stood in the doorway, a robe draped crookedly over his portly body, his sparse white hair mussed and lying at odd angles on his head like dead grass in summer.

"What the hell do you want?"

On the large bed inside the plush room, a terrified woman was holding a thick quilt up to her chin.

"Close the goddamn door," Slocum ordered the glowering man. "She has no part in this."

"How dare you break into this house like a common criminal," Proctor spat. "Now tell me what you want and get out."

"The judge has just ordered the release of your wife out of that hospital where you imprisoned her. I want you to start paying her five hundred dollars a week and give her this house."

"Are you crazy?"

"Next, I want you to give your daughter Katrina three hundred dollars a week so she can raise your grandson."

"That half-breed bastard was the son of sin when my worthless daughter made love with those heathen bastards."

"Shut up," Slocum said. "No more talk like that about your daughters."

"I'll have you killed, you—you son of a bitch."

"No, you tried that already. You have no army left to take your orders."

"I'll find them."

"They're gone, either dead or run away. It's over."

"You won't get away with this," Proctor sneered.

"You have no choice but to agree. Next time," Slocum warned, "I may put a rattlesnake in your bed."

"Tell him you'll do it! He's a madman!" Dolores screamed from the room, obviously listening through the door. "Promise him . . ." Her words seemed to be coming from terror more for her own safety than for his.

"All right. All right. I'll do it. What else do you expect of me?"

"I expect you to act like a businessman and settle your debts. Pay the ransom to the man who rescued your daughters."

"What else?"

"When Elania marries Fred Golden, I expect you to behave like a doting father and give her away cheerfully to the man she loves. And I expect you to give them a *generous* wedding present—money. Got that?"

The bedroom door opened, and Dolores stepped out. She linked her arm through Proctor's defiantly.

"Oh, my darling," she said, "this man is a killer. Do what he says."

"I'd listen to her," Slocum called out as he walked down the stairs and left. "If you don't, I'll be waiting for you."

12

Slocum met Camilla the day after her release. Diego's wife had taken her to their house for her safety, and the man sent word for Slocum to come meet her. Mrs. Proctor wanted to thank him personally.

He rode to the address in Santa Fe and dismounted at the large house. His horse hitched, he went up and knocked on the door. A maid answered and politely asked his business.

"I'm here to see Mrs. Proctor. My name is Slocum."

"Oh yes, sir. Miss Camilla is looking forward to meeting you. Come with me." She took his hat, and then led him down a hall. "Miss Camilla, Mr. Slocum is here."

A tall blond woman rose from the chair. He immediately saw the resemblance to her daughters.

"Good day, ma'am."

She quickly joined him and offered her hand. "Oh, so nice to meet you, sir. I understand you are the reason I am out of that horrible place."

He took her hand and held it for a moment. "It's a pleasure to meet you, too, ma'am."

When he looked down in her eyes, they were wet. "I—I feared I would be there the rest of my life. Oh, I am eternally grateful to everyone who worked so hard to get me out. Mr. Golden told me that you were the force behind that effort."

"Diego's wife and your own friends were the ones who saved you."

"My daughters are in hiding?"

"Elania is here in Santa Fe. We have her in a secure place so no one can get their hands on her. I am certain when she learns that you're free, she will come to see you. Katrina is still at the convent. She could have come out but she chose not to. Her son is in an orphanage here."

"Her son?" Camilla gasped.

"Yes, she has a son."

"You're a grandmother," Diego's wife said cheerfully.

"I want to see them both. Why did she stay there?"

"She hasn't talked since they were kidnapped. Elania can tell you about it. She's working now to overturn your husband's order and to adopt the boy."

Camilla blinked at him in disbelief. "You mean he had our grandson taken from her?"

"Yes. He made her sign away all her rights to the child," Slocum said.

"He has gone crazy. He lives with some woman, they say."

"I don't believe he lives with her. But she is his mistress. Her name is Dolores."

"Oh my. I'd like to kill her if she was the one who told him to put me away."

"He didn't need any help. He has turned into a bitter old man who only wants his own way and has no compassion for anyone, even his family."

"I'm sorry I ever married him. I plan to divorce him at once and be done with him."

"This entire matter is not over. Golden intends to get

you, your daughters, and your grandson the financial support that you all deserve."

"The attorney mentioned that to me. That would be heavenly. Now tell me about you. You hardly dress like a man involved in business or law. You look more like you might be a rancher."

"I am none of those things. Just someone who was able to be of assistance to your family."

She nodded. "How can I get to know you better?"

"At another time, another place, maybe. But I don't stay long in any one place."

"I would make a real effort to meet you, sometime, someplace. You know a woman who has been spurned as I have would like to find a small island of pleasure, even for a short time."

"I'm flattered," he said. "You're a very attractive woman, but I have plans to return to Texas as soon as I collect the ransom money your husband owes my friend. Colonel McKee gave the Indians supplies worth a lot of money to get your girls away from the hands of their captors."

"I just don't understand my husband's violent reaction. They're still his daughters." She looked lost.

"I'll never understand how he could imprison a lovely lady like you."

Camilla blushed. "Thank you, sir. If I can ever do anything for you, just contact me."

"I will. I'm pleased you survived, Camilla." She rose, and he kissed her on the cheek then left the house.

He mounted his horse and rode back to Consuelo's place in the junipers. He came off Pecos Road and loped through the head-high evergreens on the trail. Such a nice lady, he thought. Proctor was crazy to put her away.

As he reined up at the jacal, he noticed two strange horses hitched in back. He stopped his horse and swung him aside so he would be unseen from the area of the adobe structure. What the hell was going on? He dismounted, hitched his horse out of sight, and drew his rifle out of its scabbard. The next step was for him to see who was at her place. If they did anything to hurt her—he blew his breath out his nose—he'd damn sure settle with them.

To avoid being discovered, he swung to the west and came in from that direction. He loosened the girths on the strange horses so anyone trying to mount would turn the saddles over. He couldn't see anyone. They must be inside. Damn, if they—

There was someone he didn't know standing in the doorway. Another man was coming out dragging Consuelo by the arm. Slocum raised the Winchester and looked through the buckhorn sights at the man holding her.

The pair of kidnappers were going to take her with them and were craning their heads around for sight of any interference. The man holding her arm saw him. At the same moment, he realized he was using his gun arm to drag her with him. Slocum's bullet struck him in the chest and his knees buckled. Consuelo fell aside and the other man shot wildly, but Slocum's second bullet stopped him as well.

He was at her side in an instant. Getting on his knees, he set the rifle aside and asked her, "Are you all right?"

"I think so." She blinked her wet eyes and shook her head. "Sorry I couldn't warn you that they were here."

"Who are they?" he asked.

"I never saw them before." She went inside to get a brush for her hair. She returned, pulling out the tangles with long strokes.

He knelt by the first man. He wasn't breathing. Slocum went through his pockets, finding thirty pesos and a note in pencil that read:

He lives with a woman named Consuelo. Her place is south of the road that goes to Pecos. She has no children and lives alone. Except he stays there. She has no house address and is in those junipers. Kill him and I don't care what you do with her, but she doesn't need to be able to talk about it. Savvy? I will have your money tonight for his demise. Meet me at my warehouse. I will be there about eight o'clock, but if I am late, wait for me. I will pay you a hundred dollars when the job is done.

Proctor

"What did it say?" she asked.

"Proctor told this man he'd pay him a hundred dollars to kill me, and to hurt you, too."

She frowned at him, shaking her head. "That bastard hasn't learned a damn thing, has he?"

"No, he hasn't."

He turned his attention to the other man, who was trying to talk. "I got a—wife in Laredo. Her name is Sally Raines. Tell—tell her I died in a horse wreck trying to get back to her—tell her . . ."

"Why tell her anything?" Consuelo asked in disgust.

"I doubt I will. Guess he simply wanted one thing in his life done right."

The man had ten dollars on him and a worn-out letter to Jake Raines from his wife, Sally, showing on the envelope that it had been forwarded six times. In badly scribbled writing, Slocum could only read she wanted him to come home.

She shook her head. "Well, he isn't going to."

"I need to meet Proctor tonight at the warehouse."

"Take me with you." She shuddered, hugging her arms. "I don't want to be here alone, without you, after today."

"They didn't rape you, did they?"

"No, but they planned to do it. That was all they could talk about besides getting you. I almost told them I had the clap so they wouldn't. But then I figured they'd kill me instead."

He hugged her in his arms. "I'm sorry."

He rocked her back and forth, and she laughed, looking up at him. "What will we do with their bodies?"

"I guess after we settle with Proctor tonight, take them to the sheriff."

"Won't he ask lots of questions?"

"What else can we tell him? They kidnapped you, threatened to rape you, then shot at me."

"Do you have someone we can trust and that will tell him we are being truthful? You can't haul dead bodies into town and not draw attention."

"You're right. And it's our word against theirs. If we leave them somewhere after midnight, the only ones who'll see us will be old drunks."

He raised her chin up and kissed her. Her arms went around his neck as she stood on her toes. "This will be a lot better than taking their bodies to town," she said, smiling.

Then he swept her up in his arms and carried her inside. When he put her on her feet, she began to undress. "Lots better."

It was after sundown when they left the two horses with the bodies bound over them hitched in a deserted alley. They hurried over to the dark warehouse, their saddle horses hitched at the rack so Proctor would think they belonged to his two hired killers. The two of them waited in the shadows. Still no Proctor came. Someone must have warned him, Slocum decided, or he took a powder, not wanting to pay.

After he didn't show up, they took the blanket-covered outlaws' bodies, still tied over their saddles, downtown, hitched the two ponies in the middle of a horse-crowded hitch rail, and slipped out. Consuelo had led their horses

around the corner to wait. When Slocum joined her and
swung into his own saddle, they rode slowly up the dark
street. Then when they were farther out from the square,
they trotted their mounts back to her place.

Where was Proctor? Why hadn't he shown up to pay
the killers? Maybe he was covering his ass in case those
boys slipped up. No telling. They'd learn more in the
morning.

After the horses were unsaddled and in the pen and fed,
Slocum swept Consuelo up in his arms.

"Now I like that kinda warning," she said.

"What's that?"

"Well, every time you pick me up in your arms, you
take me to bed and we have fun. But at least I am warned.
My old man use to come up behind me, then whisper in
my ear, 'Bitch, get your clothes off. I'm gonna fuck you.' "

"Where did you find him?"

"Oh, in a cantina one night. I was sixteen, and he was
twenty-five, he said. Told me he had a big ranch and had
never been married. It turned out he was almost forty, he'd
been married four times, and had plenty of mistresses
besides. His little bastards were all over New Mexico. He
had a fake priest marry us and we had a honeymoon that
night in this jacal. I thought I was married to a wonderful
man, but when the sun came up, I decided I was the biggest
fool in the territory. There was no going back. I was already
a ruined woman and then all I could do was become a *puta*.
When I finally left him, I tried that and they fired me. I was
too dumb to even become a whore. He told me this, too,
when we were in bed. If I had not found you, I might have
hung myself."

"No, no. You are a good lover. You'll find yourself a
good man when I have to leave."

"Soon?"

"When I get McKee's money from Proctor, I need to
go back."

"Oh. When do you expect him to pay you?"

"As soon as I find him, I hope. Then I have one more thing I must do."

"What is that?"

"Find the man who murdered McKee's men."

"And you will. Now hurry and undress," she said, anxious to have him in bed with her again.

"I am. I am."

"What will I do without you, *hombre*?"

He slipped between her raised knees and sank his erection into her. She was sweet, so sweet.

Slocum was back in town the next morning. The newspaper boy was hawking a headline news story on the square, shouting. "Extra! Extra! Wanted outlaws found dead! Texas highwaymen found tied over their horses on the square!"

Hell, Slocum swore to himself. Those bastards had bounties on their head and he was worried about the local law raising hell about him shooting them. Consuelo would laugh about that when he told her.

He reached Proctor's large mercantile store and went inside. A man in a suit stopped him with a pad of paper and a pencil. "We aren't open today. We're taking inventory for the new owner."

"He's all right," a woman said, coming around the counter. It was Camilla, dressed in a new green outfit that showed off her ample bustline and trim hips. Her blond hair was pinned up, and she looked very appealing for a woman in her early forties.

"Hello, ma'am," Slocum said, tipping his hat. "It's a surprise to see you here."

"The judge ruled that this business was mine as well as Harvey's, and that he had not done me right and had, obviously, broken the law. He left yesterday before they could serve him with a warrant for his arrest."

"He hired two men to kill me at the place I was staying. They tried yesterday."

She nodded. "And their horses carried them back up on the square last night?"

"Yes, they did. Do you know where he'll go?"

"I have no idea. He did not clean out this safe. I've had guards here since the judge gave his orders to stop any attempt for him to do that."

"He must have had other places where he kept money."

"No doubt. But there is plenty here for me to keep the business going. I am in your debt, sir. I understand that he owes you a thousand dollars for the return of the girls."

"He owes it to Colonel Gill McKee. I brought the girls and came to collect it for him."

"He's a very lucky man to have you. No one would have succeeded at getting that money from my husband. I am prepared to pay it for the safe return of my girls. Come with me."

"Thank you, ma'am."

"Oh, and my younger daughter is coming home. Her son is at my house now. I am so pleased about that—I hope this will help her find her voice. And Golden is going to marry Elania, who sends you her thanks."

"You've been very busy," he said, following her into the office.

She turned and smiled. "Yes, and I know I'd not be here today except for one man's assistance. Yours."

"No, you had friends."

She went back and closed the door with the frosted window, obviously for more privacy. Then sitting down on a corner of the desk, she looked appraisingly at him. "I'm going to be quite frank with you."

"Go ahead."

"I need eight weeks to line up this business and get it to where Elania and her new husband can handle it. Then

I want to meet you somewhere. I'd like to spend a few months with you. They say it is cool down on the Gulf, like in Galveston, in the summer. What if we spent, say, six weeks down there—you and me. I have no intention of getting anything from you except fun and pleasure."

"Two months from now in Galveston, huh?"

"Yes. Can you be there?" She was squatting down in front of the safe and counting out money. "I've already paid Diego the money you borrowed. There is another five hundred in this for you to get down there on and, of course, the colonel's ransom money."

Slocum looked into the safe and exclaimed, "That son of a bitch. Hell, woman, this is enough money to choke a horse. He had plenty of cash yet he ran the three of you off?"

"Thank goodness Harvey wasn't smart enough to hide all of it, was he?"

Slocum swept her up in his arms and kissed her. Her blue eyes looked shocked then she shut them while he kissed her long and hard. No doubt about it. She was vulnerable as hell to his affections after her long term in the institution. The dress rustled like falling leaves when he took it off her. The corset had to be unlaced in the back, and his hands slid in from behind it to cup her firm breasts.

She was panting by then. Throwing her restraining undergarment aside, she turned to hug him. "Don't look at me."

"Why not? You're lovely."

She sucked in her breath again and hugged him hard. "I feel like a teenage girl again."

"Be one then." And she did.

After their tryst, he helped her replace her girdle, and she kissed him.

"I'm really serious about Galveston," she said.

"If I am not there to meet you, I'll be coming."

"I'll be staying at the Bressler Hotel."

"I can remember that." He pulled the lacing tight and she held her breath until he tied it off. Then he spanked her playfully and drew laughter from her.

"If you can't come, I'll understand."

"I'll be out of touch most of the time until then, but I'll be there."

Her hand smoothed his beard stubble. "I do feel like a woman again."

"I need to gather my things and get back to Texas."

"I understand."

He went by to talk to Deveroe. They met in a back booth.

"Can you find me several tough men in a day?"

"How many do you need?"

"Three. I'll pay them a hundred a man for about a month's work. "

"Where're you going?"

"Texas."

"There's not a lot of work here. I think I can find them."

"We can meet here tonight. Leave in the morning."

"So you're going back?"

Slocum nodded. "There's an outlaw out there, murdered some of McKee's men. I intend to find him and his henchmen. Do you know where Proctor went?"

Deveroe shook his head. "He hightailed it. But I really liked the mystery of the two dead killers."

"The law got the rewards."

"Sorry, or I'd have warned you. I had no idea how he got hold of them. He really wanted you gone."

"His stupidity cost him a fortune." Slocum shook his head. "The women now have control of his business and money. He's nowhere to be found, they say."

"Really brazen, how he had his wife declared insane." Deveroe was still shocked at the thought. "I'll have those men here at seven tonight."

"Good." He left Deveroe and rode out to Consuelo's. She rushed out to greet him. "You find Proctor?"

"No, he left. No one knows where he went. I'm going back to Cap Rock and end the problems out there with King and his gang."

"You told me about him." She held his arm possessively against her breast as they went inside. "I want you if this is my last chance."

"I have something for you."

"Oh," she said.

"Three hundred dollars."

She frowned in disbelief. "Why for me?"

"So you can dress better and find yourself a serious man."

"Oh, you don't need to do that."

"Yes, I want you to find a good man. You deserve one."

"You are so sweet." Tears began to spill down her face. "I will do as you say."

"Good."

They spent the day in her bed making love and he left her dizzy-headed to meet his new men.

In the cantina, Deveroe introduced him to the three. Jim Davis, a muscular, hard-eyed Texan in his thirties. He'd planned to return to his home state anyway, and this gave him a chance to make good money along the way. Yeager Taylor was dark, stout, and worked with explosives, he said. Temple Green had little to say but he understood they were going after some killers. Green was a thin, wiry man in his late twenties. They were to meet at the Pecos turnoff at dawn.

Slocum went back to Consuelo's place for the last night, and they were up before dawn, loading his packhorses and getting ready to ride. He hugged her, kissed her tears, and told her she was pretty. Then he rode out. He had the men he needed and they could move swiftly back to the fort.

Aside from a few thunderstorms that passed quickly, they reached the fort in a week. Everyone was worn out upon their arrival, and Slocum called for a couple days' rest for men and beasts.

McKee was tickled to see them and agreed to pay his hired men. He poured the whiskey and they raised their glasses to him. Slocum's back ached some from the pressing ride, but he wasn't in a whiskey-drinking mood. In the kitchen, Willow told him to go to his old cabin and get some rest. The fire had been built up, the room was already heated, there was hot bathwater, and she leaned over to whisper, "Butter Fly is there."

He nodded. Who the hell was she? He thanked her and walked over to the jacal.

When he walked through the door, a tall Indian woman in her twenties dressed in buckskins smiled at him and stood up.

"Butter Fly?" he asked.

She nodded. "You met me before. I was at the lodges when you came by and told us to come here. You did not see me then but I saw you. The man I was with died after we came here. He was ill. Willow told me all you have done for them, and I am to show you a good time." Her words came one at a time as if she needed to be proper and be sure she used the right ones.

"I guess a bath would suit me."

"That is the way of the white man?" she asked.

"I guess. To be clean and to shave."

"Do you kiss your women?"

"Have you ever been kissed by a man?"

"No."

He took her in his arms and kissed her. She smiled when he stopped. "I see why she likes you."

He shed his coat. "What will you do without your man?"

"When the thaw comes, I will go back to my people at

the reservation and find a man to live with. Living out here is too hard. There are less buffalo left than we thought. In our lifetime they have gone from many to so few."

He nodded, undressed, and stepped into the half barrel of bathwater. She removed her fringe shirt and put it carefully aside. Then she began to wash him. Her pear-shaped breasts swung with her efforts, and they stopped to kiss a few times. Nothing wild, but when he got out, she got in and bathed, too, as he dried himself off.

With the shaving cup, he used the hog bristle brush and applied the lather to his face. Then he used his folded blade razor to carefully scrape his face of the beard stubble. Butter Fly was out drying herself when he finished and rinsed the blade off.

After he rinsed his face, he dried it, and she came over to stand naked before him. Her copper brown skin looked flawless. On the slender side, she looked beautiful in the candlelight.

He had to have her. This time her mouth came to life and they soon were deep in passion's spell, which led them to bed and more intimacy. With his dick in her firm vagina, they rode to the top of the world in a whirlpool of fever and need until he exploded inside her. She fainted away, and he stiffened his arms to support his weight so he wouldn't crush her.

"Come back," she murmured. "Your body feels so good on top of me. I have been a long time without a man. Even a longer time away from a strong one—and the white man's kissing is fun."

He laughed. "Do you wish to do it again?"

"Yes." She smiled up at him and her dark eyes danced with the diamonds of her tears on her long lashes. "I never thought, in my life, that a white man would make me so crazy and also make me feel so good."

"You were just starved is all."

They stayed occupied until supper time. She dressed

and started to leave. Her hand on the door, she asked, "Should I come back?"

"Why not?"

"I will be here later. Can I tell Willow that what she said was right?"

"What's that?"

"She said, 'You will have a good honeymoon with him today.'"

He laughed. "Come back and kiss me good-bye." And she did, then she hurried off. He dressed leisurely, thinking he was the luckiest man in the world. Even in the middle of nowhere on Cap Rock, he'd found a great woman. Damn.

13

After two days of Butter Fly's company, Slocum told the men, at supper, that they'd be riding for King's camp in the morning. Juan was going along. They were all armed with Winchester repeating rifles and had lots of ammo. Yeager was in charge of loading the blasting stick bombs. The three asked him questions about King and his men over the meal.

McKee finally said, "King got him so mad last time, Slocum notched his left ear."

The men laughed and passed bowls of food around the table. Davis spoke up. "Colonel, if he's all the trouble you got up here, consider him gone."

McKee thanked him.

After another night with Butter Fly, Slocum was up before dawn. They planned to take only one packhorse and travel light. The temperature was above freezing and they rode out, cheered on by the fort crew.

Slocum told them to trot their horses. He wanted to reach King's camp by midday.

"How tough is his crew?" Davis asked.

"Mostly breeds. They probably got drunk last night. I imagine that's how he holds them."

Davis nodded. "Do they have lots of horses?"

"I don't know. We couldn't find them last time. It was just Juan and me, and I didn't want them to know I was after them. We never found their horses."

"Maybe he sent them where he had feed for them."

"That's an idea."

"You don't consider him much of a threat?"

"I never said that. He's tough or he would not have survived this long."

"You think he has his eye on taking the fort?"

Slocum nodded. "That's why he stayed out here all winter."

"I'll be glad when this is over," Davis said. "I'm going over into the panhandle and catch that new train. They've built tracks out here and then they'll take it all the way to Denver. I'm riding it back to Fort Worth."

"I may tag along," Slocum said. "They have it that far out here?"

"Yeah, they've been building on it all the time."

"Good." About noon, he had them hold up. He and Juan rode ahead and surveyed the camp from a distance with his field glasses. They saw several squaws scraping the fat from buffalo hides pegged down on the ground. One or two breeds walked around. Neither was armed, and that made Slocum think that they weren't ready for an attack.

They slipped back and told the other three that camp looked ready to be taken. They unlimbered their rifles and spread out. The squaws saw them coming and ran for cover screaming.

King came out wearing a blanket against the cool wind.

Slocum's men spread out and demanded that everyone come out unarmed. One breed must have shot his gun off inside the lodge. Jim Davis slipped off the right side of his horse and shot in the air near the front entrance.

Someone screamed, "No! No!" The breed came out with his hands up; so did others in a hurry. Slocum and his men herded them to a place where King stood looking sullen. "What the fuck is this?" he demanded.

"You murdered three of my friends who were buffalo hunting. Why?" Slocum asked, getting off his horse.

"I don't know what the fuck you're talking about."

"Yes you do."

"Where's your proof?"

"The words of a dying man—one of your men—are all the proof I need. I'm taking you back to the colonel right now."

"Like hell you are," King said, then quickly reached inside the blanket to draw his gun.

But he wasn't quick enough. Slocum drew out his Colt and shot King in the shoulder. Incredibly, he seemed impervious to the pain and managed to get off one shot, which whizzed by Slocum's ear but didn't hit it. He tried to shoot again, but Slocum fired, this time hitting the man in the chest.

"Goddamn it!" King cried, then he coughed up blood and fell forward, twitching for a moment before he lay still.

The squaws started keening and wailing.

"The rest of you have three days to get off Cap Rock or get the same treatment. Do you understand?" Slocum called out, looking around.

Somber faces nodded.

"Three days to abandon this camp, and you have no right to return."

"Mount up," he said to his men.

They obeyed and rode back to the fort. King was dead. McKee and his fort were safe.

They arrived at sundown. Slocum went to the storeroom and grabbed a pint of whiskey. Willow offered him food, but he shook his head. He went to the jacal, where Butter Fly was waiting for him. He uncorked the bottle and downed a large amount of the raw liquor.

"Can I do anything for you?"

He held out his hand to keep her seated.

"I need this liquor to take some of the edge off my mind. It's on fire." He drank again, enjoying the fire of a different kind burning a path down his body.

"What can I do to help?" she asked.

"Just be patient. This whole thing is finally over, and I have to loosen up," he said, taking still another large swig.

"You found him?"

"Yes. He won't bother anyone again."

She nodded and put her arm on his shoulder. "Kiss me, big man. I can take you away."

He complied, and it worked. All that liquor on an empty belly helped, too.

14

Juan reported that the camp was empty on the second day. All the lodges were gone. Good, thought Slocum. They'd taken him seriously. He told the three men in two more days he'd pay them and told Jim Davis he'd be ready to ride to the end of the train tracks.

"You going to Fort Worth?" Davis asked.

Slocum shook his head. "No, San Antonio." Then on to Galveston, but there was no rush. What did she say, she wanted two months?

He had about one month used up. And he had a ways to go. Besides, San Antonio was always a great place to dance with dusky women and raise hell. Then Galveston was only a hop, skip, and jump away.

When he said good-bye to McKee, the colonel paid him five hundred dollars for all his work.

"Come back again. I may need another rescue sometime."

"Sure thing." The two men shook hands.

Butter Fly looked really sad sitting on a stool and kicking her legs back and forth. "So you must go away?"

"When you have enemies that track you, you have to be on the go."

"Where will you go next?"

"Texas."

"Why there?"

"Big place. Easy to hide."

"But what will I do?" She swung her legs faster.

"Be glad I'm gone."

"No."

"I'm leaving you a hundred dollars to find a man to kiss."

She giggled. "Where will I look?"

"Maybe at Fort Sill?"

She nodded, then jumped off the stool. Bent over, she shed her fringed blouse. "Why are you not undressing?"

"I was waiting for you." He laughed and joined her.

In a few minutes they were having a rousing affair of kissing and copulation that stole their breath and threw them into a whirlpool of passion. The afternoon faded until they quit to go to supper. After the meal, they went arm in arm like drunks back to make more love.

In the early morning, Butter Fly helped him load his packhorse with his bedroll and the necessary supplies. Figuring they would be four days getting to the railroad, Davis used the other horse and they left before the sunrise glowed pink on the horizon. Slocum kissed Butter Fly good-bye and told her to find another man who liked to kiss. She laughed and shook her head. "There is no one like you. I will miss you."

He and Davis made good time, and on the third day they came upon the railroad grading crew. Following the stakes, they soon saw the awesome operation of tie-laying and then the iron tracks being spiked down. They rode past the operation to the first tent city and found food that beat their own cooking. Davis found a whore and told Slocum he'd be ready to move on at sunup.

Slocum reminded him that they needed to sell their horses so they could take the train. Jim agreed to let him sell them all, said he'd find him in the morning, and hurried off with the young prostitute. Since it was a weeknight, she'd probably agreed to a cheaper price for entertaining him all night.

Slocum sold all three horses and then took his and Davis's saddles to the temporary depot. The agent said the next train heading east left about noon the next day. He found a dry place to spread out his own bedroll and went to sleep early. He was up again early, looking for breakfast. Davis arrived shortly afterward, looking like he'd come through a knothole.

"You sell the horses?" Jim asked.

"I sold mine for forty bucks a head."

Shocked, Davis frowned at him. "What did mine bring? Damn, that was cheap."

"No, I got fifty for yours."

"Good. When does the train leave?"

Slocum gave him his money. "Noon, the freight man said."

"Maybe I'll feel better by then."

"You eating breakfast?"

"Naw, I'll get something later. You'll never believe who I seen today."

"Who?"

"That big man who was in the scandal about sticking his wife in the insane asylum—Proctor."

Slocum frowned at him. "Where?"

"He was in a card game when I saw him last night. The woman I was with had a room out back of the tent that he was playing in."

"I want that son of a bitch," Slocum said. "He sent men twice to kill me."

"We can find him. They'll know in that place where he hangs out."

· "If we have to stay over a day, I want him."

"No problem. I've got lots of time," Davis said to him.

The bartender said that Proctor had a tent north of the railroad town. It was noon before they located the tent, but it was empty.

"You reckon he saw you and left?" Davis asked him.

"Hear that train whistle?" Slocum said. "That's the last train to Fort Worth for today."

"You figure he took a powder?"

Slocum glanced around in disgust. "There ain't much here he left behind."

"Where will he go next?"

"Fort Worth, I suppose." When Slocum got there, he'd invest some time looking around for him.

"Right where I'm headed," Davis said. "Sorry, you never said you wanted him."

"No problem. We won't be far behind." Just twenty-four hours was all.

"Right."

They left on the next train at noon and arrived in Fort Worth about three the next morning. They were in the stockyards and the strong stench of the slaughterhouses hung heavy in the night air. Davis suggested the Drover's Hotel, so they took a room and slept till midday. Then they sought baths, a shave and a haircut, and put on clean clothes from their war bags.

Slocum felt naked walking around the district without the gun harness around his waist. But this was not the Wild West, and he wished for no attention from the law. Davis went one way and he went the other, hoping that Proctor had settled in playing cards in one of the many saloons. They met up in the late afternoon at the White Elephant Saloon but had no word on the man's whereabouts.

Then a man who knew Davis came by the table where they were nursing their second draft beer.

"Jim, I ain't seen you in six months. How have you been?"

"This is Hughes. I've known him for years. This is Slocum."

Slocum shook his hand and sat back down.

"You recall that big businessman in Santa Fe named Proctor?" Davis asked. It was obvious Hughes had once been in Santa Fe.

"Yeah, I saw him yesterday."

"Here?" Davis asked.

"Yeah. Funny—I wondered what he was doing here. He was over at the Johnson Slaughterhouse. I had some money coming to me from some cattle I sold them. He was in there talking to the head man. I first asked myself who he was and then I remembered him."

"Sit down and we'll buy you a beer," Slocum said. "We need more information. Do you know someone in that office who could tell us what he was up to?"

"What did he do?"

Slocum told him how Proctor had refused to pay the ransom. How he put the girls in a convent, and had his men beat Slocum up. How he'd committed his own wife to the crazy bin so he could be with his mistress. How he'd sent more men to finish Slocum off.

"There's a guy named Scott who works for them and he might tell me."

"Here's ten dollars. Work on it."

"We're staying at the Drover's," Davis added. "We need to stop him from hurting someone else."

"I'll be here tomorrow night and have all the info. Right now I know a gal that ain't booked up that wants seven bucks for me to sleep all night with her." He downed his beer in one long drink, made a loud belch, and set the mug on the table. "Thanks. See you two."

Davis nodded to Slocum. "We may have a good lead. Hughes don't lie."

"I'll take any way we can to get him pinned down." He wanted Proctor to pay for his crimes.

"I think we're going to do it." They had a third beer to celebrate.

The next day, Davis went to see a woman he knew. He came back to the Elephant that afternoon acting down.

"What's wrong?" Slocum asked.

"She wasn't glad to see me. Either she has new boyfriend or don't want me anymore."

"Hell, you cleaned up pretty good," Slocum said, shaking his head.

"She said I was un-respons-able."

"That a disease?" Slocum asked and tried not to laugh.

"No, she said it meant she couldn't count on me being there. Hell, we aren't married. And we'd had a big fight and I went to New Mexico."

"You want her bad enough?"

"Hell, yes, I wouldn't have come back here to pick cotton."

"Let me think on it. I'll figure something out." Slocum's mind began to sift through possible plans to impress her and to show her that Davis wasn't a drifter.

Hughes joined them and Slocum ordered him a beer. "What do you know?"

"Proctor wants to invest in a business in Fort Worth. He claimed he had thousands of dollars at his disposal. The Johnson family isn't interested in a partner, though."

"If that son of a bitch still has any money, part of it belongs to his family."

"Well, that's what he wants. Oh, and he's staying at the Nelson Hotel downtown."

"We can go down there and maybe confront him, can't we?" Davis said.

"Maybe," Slocum said. "We need to lure him out into our hands."

"Good idea."

"We need to send him a letter by messenger and get him to meet us at some isolated place."

"The North Fort Worth Cemetery," Hughes said and laughed. "You can go up there by taxi and take your guns along."

"We'll need them. That son of a bitch tried to have Slocum killed at least twice, maybe three times."

"Whew. I'd go loaded for bear if it was me."

Slocum agreed. "I might have to do that." He would need to know where all the money was at, or it could all be lost in some secret account.

"Could you meet him and find out where he keeps his money?"

"Me?" Hughes about swallowed his Adam's apple. "No. But I know a guy named Schade who could do it."

"How dependable is he?" Slocum asked.

"Oh, he might do it for nothing. He likes having adventures."

All Slocum knew was that his circle was growing larger. If this guy would come in on it, the number would now be four. But what could he lose?

They met at a smaller bar out of the stockyard district and Schade dropped by. Slocum told him about Proctor's trickery and that they would need his account number and the name of the bank. All he had to do was offer him a partnership, but his boss would have to know that Proctor really had the money. No hoax.

"Where will I meet him?"

"North Fort Worth Cemetery. We'll be in hiding and won't let him hurt you."

Schade was a good actor. He sounded tough enough, and Slocum said he'd pay him ten dollars for the information and fifty for the bank book.

"When you get it, you can shout. We'll be right there."

"What if he has a gun?"

"We'll take care of him. Don't risk your own life."

Schade nodded. "When do we do it?"

"Tomorrow night or it will have to wait until Monday."

"Where will we meet?" Schade asked.

"At the Elephant in a back booth," Slocum said. "Don't show off. Keep a low profile."

They shook hands on the deal and separated.

Slocum decided they needed more time to work on this deal before they sprung the trap on Proctor. No way could they simply coax him out to the graveyard, find out about his hidden bank account, and then arrest him. They also could spook him off if they went too fast. As much as he wanted Proctor behind bars, Slocum owed it to the three women to get that money he must have stashed and then take him in for the New Mexican authorities to deal with. But time might also mean more chance of their exposure and him running off.

He and Davis went back to the hotel.

"You're in deep thought about this deal?" Davis asked quietly as they walked the dark street, lit by an occasional streetlamp.

"How bad do you want this woman who's scorned you?"

"Real bad. I thought I could come back here and convince her to marry me. My dad has a place down by San Antonio. He asked me to come back home and run it. I figured if Shelly would marry me, I'd settle down."

"All right. What if we arrest Proctor and you get the credit for it? Get your name in the newspaper for tracking him down. Would that convince her you're serious enough?"

"Hey, I'm helping you, not the other way around."

"Listen, if I can get you in good with her and that's what you want, why wouldn't you use it to convince her that you're serious?"

"Why do this for me?"

"I like you. I'd like to settle down someplace myself, but I can't. So if you can use this to get her, why not?"

"What do I have to do?"

"What we're doing right now. Trap Proctor and then arrest him and you take him in. If there is as much money as I think he got away with, you could be well off with the reward from his wife for its recovery."

"Well off?"

"It might get you, say, a thousand bucks."

"Whoa, that's a lot of money."

"We haven't got it yet. But do you think you could turn her head doing this?"

"Damn, Slocum. I am serious about her. She ain't the queen of England, but I'd sure like to have her and settle down. I ain't gettin' any younger."

"Keep up your appearances with her. Don't be pushy. Then when it happens, act casual."

"Hey, you gave me a new lease on life tonight. I better get a bath, shave, and go see her tomorrow."

"Just act calm."

"Oh, I think I can do that."

In the morning, Davis went to clean up. By evening Slocum had an idea.

Schade had to send Proctor a message to meet him. They rehearsed what Schade needed to tell him—that he owned a share in his Grandpa Ralph Johnson's slaughterhouse and was ready to sell it. But they had to be quiet because his father didn't want him to sell. He'd heard that Proctor wanted to buy into that successful business, and his grandfather agreed to the sale even if it meant going against his son's wishes. If they were quiet about it, Schade could help Proctor buy in for a small fee for his part. He wanted to do something else with his life.

They met in at a restaurant uptown. Schade gave them the report later that night. "He really wants into that business. He acted cool enough but I know he's pleased to have me helping him. I made a list of the things he wants to know before the deal goes further."

"Can we find all this out?" Slocum asked after looking at the list.

"Hey, for ten bucks I can have it done tomorrow," Hughes said.

"I'm going to count on that," Slocum replied.

They returned the next night and went over the things Proctor wanted and the answers.

When they finished, Schade nodded. "They have a damn good business, don't they?"

"Yes, and I can see why they don't need his money," Slocum said. "Schade, you now have all the answers he wants."

"Yeah, and I'm sure looking forward to fooling the bastard."

"Now you need to tell him that the old man wants to be damn sure he has the money to do this and where it's at or he won't talk to him."

"What if Proctor balks?" Schade asked.

"Then we'll tell him no deal," Slocum said. "I think he wants in badly enough to agree."

"Meet him in the cemetery after dark on the north side in that grove of trees," Davis instructed. "I think we can surround the place easily there."

"We need to be out of sight and ready to spring the trap when we find out the specifics of the money. Schade, you need to give him a cigar and light one for yourself when you get the information."

"I can do that."

"If he gets riled or anything, you drop the deal and we'll come on the run."

"I may become a detective," Schade said. "If Slocum will coach me."

They laughed.

"Guys, if we get lucky and pull this off," Slocum told them in a low voice, "I guarantee you'll have some nice money in your pockets. I got a wire today. The sheriff in Santa Fe told Proctor's wife that he would send two deputies here to get him as soon as he knew the authorities here had him in custody. So we'll have no problem having him held. If we can learn the whereabouts of his money, we've got the frosting on the cake."

They nodded. In the next twenty-four hours, they would know if their plan worked or not. Slocum knew lots of things rode on the deal. But unless Proctor found out it was hoax, they should make it work. And the man's greed also helped grease the tracks for them.

When he and Davis went back, they talked softly along the way. "How are things going?" Slocum asked.

"Better. You mean with my girl Shelly, don't you?" Davis said.

"That's the other game we got going, isn't it?"

"I asked her yesterday if she would go down to San Antonio and look at the family ranch."

"And?"

"She said she would but not to expect that would change her mind."

"Hey, you've made some progress."

"I told her I couldn't explain what I was doing but I was gainfully employed for the moment."

"She understand that?"

Davis nodded. "I think when she meets my parents and sees the ranch, I'll stand a chance."

"Good. In twenty-four hours, we'll know a lot more."

"Hey, I appreciate what you're doing for me. I guess I was suspicious at first. Now it's making sense. We're going to win."

"Time will tell."

"You're right, but I'm sure feeling better on all fronts. Thanks for taking me along."

The setup was made. Proctor was to meet Schade at eight o'clock in the graveyard. The cards had been dealt.

By nightfall, Slocum, Davis, and Hughes were hiding in the cemetery in the area where Schade was to meet Proctor. When it was time to arrest Proctor, Schade would give the signal by lighting a cigar.

On the ground about a hundred feet from the point where Schade waited, Slocum had a good view through the shadow of trees. The moon had begun to rise, and when the three-quarter globe provided some light, it would be easier to see.

A single-horse taxi cab came clopping onto the grounds. The .44 in his fist, belly down on the ground, Slocum could hear Proctor tell the taxi driver to pull over and that he would not be long. The man drove the horse to one side.

Slocum couldn't hear the conversation between Schade and Proctor. His heart pounding in his chest was the loudest thing he could hear. The time passed slower than cold molasses. Then Schade struck a match and Slocum was on his feet.

"Get your hands in the air or die," he shouted. "This is the law speaking."

Schade had his hands up and Proctor joined him.

"What the fuck is this?" Proctor demanded.

"I don't know," Schade answered.

Hughes was there already and had disarmed Proctor. Davis told the cab driver to stay there.

Proctor blinked in shock at Slocum. "Are you behind this?"

Ignoring him, Slocum turned to Schade. "Well?"

"He has two keys to two safe-deposit boxes in his vest pocket. He showed them to me. He planned to show me the money tomorrow at the bank."

"What the hell is this?"

"Oh, your wife Camilla sends her regards and was sorry that she could not be here for a reunion." Slocum took the keys from Proctor's vest. "Are you ready to go back to New Mexico and stand trial?"

"Listen, I can pay all of you—"

"How much?"

"Over a hundred thousand dollars."

"No thanks," Slocum said.

"Damn you. It was my mistake. I should have killed you myself."

"Hiring cheap help must have been the problem. Davis, you take him to the marshal and have him held for the Santa Fe sheriff, who has warrants for his arrest on felony charges. Hughes, go along and be certain he doesn't try to get away. We'll meet at the usual place at eleven tomorrow morning."

The First Bank of Texas opened at 9 a.m. Fifteen minutes later, Slocum entered the building and presented the keys to the clerk. The clerk told Slocum to follow him. Inside the brass-fronted safety-deposit box room, the man used his master key and the keys Slocum handed to him to unlock two boxes.

Slocum thanked the man and began packing the satchel he brought with stacks and stacks of paper money. The job finally complete, he wondered how much was in the suitcase. It was heavy enough.

He shut the doors on the deposit boxes and removed both of his keys. Then he walked out of the vault and thanked the man. On the street he hailed a taxi and went to the Wells Fargo Office four blocks away. There he talked to the manager about transferring the money to Camilla Proctor's account in Santa Fe at the New Mexico National Bank, and the man said they would need to count the money.

"Good. Do it. Just make sure it gets there."

"Oh, we're totally insured, but we must know the amount we are handling."

"Okay, I'll be back this afternoon for the receipt showing the full amount and indicating that you've sent it."

"Very good, sir. Do you have any idea how much is there?" He motioned to the satchel.

"Two hundred thousand, maybe more."

"Good heavens. How did you get that?"

"A man stole it from his family business. I'm returning it."

"They must be very pleased. Here is a receipt for the satchel saying it's worth 'about two hundred thousand dollars.' When you come back, I will have counted it, sent, and will give you another receipt with the exact amount."

"The women who receive it will be very pleased. Thank you, sir. See you later."

Next, he sent a telegram to Camilla. He told her he had more money to send her from Proctor's hidden stash. He also told her to send him three bank drafts: Jim Davis, one thousand; C. Hughes, five hundred; and Mark Schade, five hundred. He would distribute them. He would send her another telegram indicating the exact amount of the new stash of money once it had been counted. There was going to be lots of money for her family.

Slocum and the three others met and had lunch at the Elephant. He announced that the money was being counted at the Wells Fargo Office and would soon be heading to Santa Fe.

"How much?" Schade asked, busily eating his soup.

"I am guessing it to be close to a quarter of a million dollars."

Schade about choked on the hot liquid he was swallowing. "He stole that much?"

"He had plan B, I guess. He had a nice-looking mistress. Hell knows where she ended up. And we have no idea if this is even all of his money. His wife didn't know how much money he had in the store safe. I guess he was lying to her all the time about his profitability. She had many friends among the upper crust of Santa Fe, and those ladies told the judge to get her out of the crazy house. When she was out, the pieces of Proctor's life began to fall like dominoes.

"Jim discovered him at the end of the Fort Worth-to-Denver tracks over by Tularosa and he beat us leaving for Fort Worth by twenty-four hours. But Jim found him here and that's when we hired you two."

"You should have been there when Jim told those reporters his story about capturing Proctor in the cemetery," Hughes said. "Man, he told them how he coaxed him out there so no one else would get hurt or shot in case that Proctor went to shooting at him. He told them all the charges that were awaiting him in New Mexico. And what a scallywag Proctor was. They loved it. He had his wife put away, shipped his kidnapped daughters off to a convent in shame, and even had his bastard grandson put in an orphanage. They were ready to lynch him down at the sheriff's office today."

Hughes burst out laughing. Davis seemed a little embarrassed by all the attention.

"We did well," Slocum said. "There's no doubt about that. You fellows will soon be a little richer. I'm grateful, and so are the women. If you ever need a job in New Mexico, all you have to do is tell them who you are—the men who nailed Harvey Proctor."

"Where are you headed next?" Hughes asked Slocum.

"Oh, I have several places to go."

"If you ever need me, just holler," Hughes said. "I'll come a-running. Whew! I'm going to my mom and dad's this next week and buy me some cows so someday I can own a ranch. They'll be shocked I saved anything. Davis, what are you going to do?"

"Build a house on my dad's spread out in the hill country."

"What for?"

"I hope my woman will marry me, and then we'll go run the ranch. My dad's getting too old to do it."

"You sound serious," Hughes said.

"It's up to her now."

"And Slocum's sugar-footin' away." Hughes laughed and raised his mug of beer. "Here's to us all."

The party broke up. Slocum paid the bill for the food, then he and Jim walked back to the hotel to pack.

"Do you think she'll marry you?"

"I hope so. I told her I'd build our own house down there."

"No idea what she'll tell you?" he asked Davis.

"I'm thinking she may do it. I hope the newspaper story impresses her some. Hell, I tried."

"You damn sure did."

They were almost to the hotel when a woman who was sitting on the hotel stairs jumped up and called to Jim.

"Is that her?" Slocum asked under his breath.

Jim perked up and hurried to hug her.

By the time he got to them, she was crying and they were kissing.

"Ah, Slocum, this here is Shelly."

She wiped at her wet eyes. "Nice to meet you, Mr. Slocum. I'm so glad you brought him back to Texas for me."

"It was no problem, ma'am. Are you two fixing to get hitched?"

"Yes, we are, if he doesn't change his mind."

"Naw, he won't," Slocum said.

She laughed. "You sure sound certain."

"Good luck, you two. I need to move on. Thanks, Jim. I never could have done it without you."

They shook hands, and two hours later, Slocum was on board the Texas Central passenger train to Houston with a ticket to get off in San Antonio. With three weeks to kill before he was to meet his rich lady friend in Galveston, he planned to relax in the Alamo City. Something about the place attracted him time after time. The pretty brown-skin girls were one thing; the gentle music and dancing in the evening around the area of the old church-fort were another.

He could gather his wits again in such a soothing environment. That was what he looked forward to when he took a seat in the middle of the car, behind a young woman with a baby in her lap.

At first, he didn't paid her much mind but soon found himself in a conversation with her, and he turned around the empty seat in front of her so he could sit down to continue their conversation face-to-face.

Joan Briscoe was her name. Her boy was Samuel Colt Briscoe. He guessed her to be close to twenty. She had blue eyes and light brown, almost blond hair, and a nice figure. He soon learned she was going to live at her family's home place while her husband took a herd of cattle to the Kansas markets that summer. In the fall when he came home, he was going to come get her and his son and they were going to look for a new ranch for themselves. A very nice story. She asked him about the trail north that her husband was on by this time.

When the train stopped in Waco, Slocum got off on the depot platform, found the three of them some food, and bought a newspaper. The headlines screamed about a thwarted bank robbery up at Denison. When he was back on the train, Joan offered to pay him for the food, but he refused, and held the boy for her while she ate.

After she finished eating her fried chicken and bread, he ate his food and looked at the newspaper while she nursed her baby.

He read that earlier on Tuesday three then unknown men rode into Denison, and at midafternoon pulled up masks and charged into the North Texas Bank on Ranger Avenue to rob it. In an exchange of gunfire with the bank president, Phillip Eubanks, and teller Rupert Cornelius, one of the robbers was shot dead. His name was Henry Pike. As the other two escaped to the street, the town marshal shot and killed James Erwin Briscoe of Fort Worth, a gang member. The third man escaped—his name was believed to be Harry Court. A reward of five hundred was offered dead or alive for this Harry Court's capture.

Slocum looked at the woman across from him. The clack of the train wheels on the joints pounded much louder. The sway of the car rocked them from side to side. How could he tell her that her husband had not been on a cattle drive at all, and that he was not coming back for her this fall? How did he get himself into such a situation?

He drew a deep breath. "Is your husband's middle name Erwin?"

She blinked her blue eyes. "Yes, have you met him?"

"No, ma'am, but you better read this newspaper. Hand me little Sam."

Looking lost, she traded the boy for the newspaper. "Oh, no . . ."

When she looked up, the color had drained from her complexion. "These are the men he was going to Kansas with. Why would they do this?"

"I have no answer as to the why of it, ma'am."

Tears spilled down her face. "I'm so sorry, sir. I had no idea. I thought they'd sold the cattle already and I—I was going home. Where did they bury him?"

"A pauper's grave, I imagine."

"But how could he have done this?"

Slocum handed her his kerchief then he bounced the boy a little on his leg. "How long did you know him?"

"Two, maybe three years. I met him at a dance. He worked for a few ranchers, then he said he was heading up a herd. His parents have a ranch west of San Antonio. I'll have to tell them if they haven't heard. What will I do?"

"I don't know your circumstances, ma'am."

"I have a six-month-old son, and I'm the widow of an—an outlaw."

"Can you stay with your parents?"

"Yes, but what will I do—oh, I don't know what I'll do."

"Where are your parents at?"

"They have a ranch in the hill country."

"We can rent a buckboard and I can take you up there."

"Oh, I could not impose on you—"

"Do you have anyone to help you?"

"No."

"Then I'll take you up there myself."

"But you have your own life."

"Don't worry, I can handle both."

"Well, I don't know . . . imposing on a stranger. How will it look?"

"I'm not sure but you need help. I can get you to where you want to be."

The train reached the depot in San Antonio in the middle of the night. He made certain her trunks were on the dock along with his saddle and war bag. She handed him Samuel Colt and went to use the facilities. "I'll be right back."

It was the last time he saw her that night. He and Samuel were left on the San Antonio Depot platform waiting for his mother to return. The longer he waited, the more jittery he felt, and he began walking and bouncing his newfound buddy. Something was obviously wrong. He finally went inside and asked the agent if he'd seen a woman in a brown dress.

"Yeah, she met two men and they left in a buckboard together."

"Buckboard? Did she look like she was being kidnapped?"

"Well, she didn't seem to know either of them."

"Easy, Sam. We'll find her." It would help if I knew her family's name.

First item, he needed to find someone to babysit Sam. The infant wasn't happy about the absence of his mother. A city cop sent him by taxi to the house address of a Mary Dolin. He woke a large buxom blond woman who swept her ample hair back over her shoulder.

The woman said she would care for him. She and Sam hit it off though he needed an immediate changing. The taxi man unloaded the trunk that contained Sam's things. Slocum had left Joan's trunk and his war bag and saddle at the train station. The woman changed Sam's diaper and told Slocum she would feed and care for him until he returned. He paid her ten dollars, and she looked pleased.

"I believe his mother was kidnapped. I'll be back when I know more."

"Thank you. He will be well cared for."

"Much obliged," Slocum said. This woman sounded very trustworthy and sincere.

He left her place and decided to get a hotel room to rest a few hours. His mind was blank from exhaustion and concern for the little guy and his mother. After a few hours of troubled sleep, he went downtown to the main police department. They knew nothing about the disappearance of the woman.

"One minute she was there and asked me to hold the baby. Next, the agent told me two men had herded her off in a buckboard. I had to find a woman to watch her baby."

"Why didn't you report her missing then?" the officer at the desk asked.

"I had not had any sleep in twenty-four hours. And I had to find a woman to care for the baby. You damn sure don't want him down here."

"What was her name?"

"Mrs. Joan Briscoe. She had just learned that her husband, who she thought was driving cattle north to Kansas, had been shot to death in a muddled bank robbery up in Denison."

"I knew I'd heard that name."

"Do you know where his parents live?"

The deskman shook his head.

"She would never have left that boy with me unless she was kidnapped. She's a fine mother."

"Then where did she disappear to? She got rid of her son by giving him to you, and was going to hide out."

"Quit supposing. Name some men who live here that might have wanted her for something."

"Did she have any money from another crime they might have wanted?"

"You have all the information I know. I'm going to look for her and I'm going to be looking for his parents. Someone will know them."

"Meanwhile, where are you staying?" the deskman asked.

"Hotel San Carlos."

"Check back in with me in two days. Sign your name on this paper."

"You can check every day at the San Carlos bar." Slocum signed it and left. Then he went back to the Alamo district. More than likely her kidnappers came out of that area because that was where, in the city, most of the cowboys and ranchers usually stayed.

Who'd rented a buckboard yesterday from a livery? He asked each stable about renters in the area, and it was afternoon before he found a likely renter at Price's Livery. A white-bearded gentleman named Jenkins gave a description of a pair of men in their late twenties who'd acted upset the day before when renting a team and buckboard.

He'd made them put up two hundred dollars up for security, because he thought they were acting shady. They said John Carson and Eli Campbell were their names. They were supposed to have already brought the buckboard back, so it was overdue. Slocum decided to wait to see who returned the rig for their deposit just in case they did come back. That was a large sum, and he decided that unless they were real rich, they'd want it back. Across the street from the livery a Hispanic vendor woman made him some lunch on a small cooker. About the time she got his beans and meat wrapped in a large tortilla, a boy of twelve or so arrived in a buckboard. Slocum rushed back across the street to the livery.

Jenkins began looking around, waving for him.

"That's my rig," he said, indicating the outfit. "I don't know this boy."

The barefoot youth in his early teens tied off the reins, jumped off the rig, and held out his hand to Jenkins. "Mister, Big Jim said he wanted his two hundred bucks back or he'd bust my ass wide open."

Jenkins nodded for Slocum to interrogate him.

"Who's Big Jim?" Slocum asked.

"Big Jim Lansberry."

"Where's he live at?"

"Over on Stack Street."

"Was the woman crying when you left them?" Slocum asked him.

The boy's face went white as a sheet. He swallowed hard.

"Do you know her?" Slocum asked.

"No."

"Have they been treating her mean?"

Numb-looking, the boy nodded.

Slocum said, "I've got a twenty-dollar gold piece. You take me where she's at and it's yours."

The boy started to panic. "I need his deposit first or he'll kill me."

"I'm giving it to this man," Jenkins said, indicating Slocum. "He can give it to him. You sure won't get hurt. He won't let Big Jim hurt you."

"He said he'd bust my ass if I didn't get right back."

Slocum shook his head. "I won't let him do that. Jenkins, loan me a pistol. I'll handle this matter."

The bearded man rushed inside and came back with a short-barrel Sheriff model .45 Colt. "It's loaded."

Slocum thanked him. He slipped the handgun in his waistband and the two hurried off. Three blocks away from the livery, the boy pointed to an adobe jacal halfway down the street. "They're gonna be mad at me for bringing you here, mister. I know them."

"I can handle them. Are they drunk?"

He made a quick nod. "Kin I have that money now?"

"No, you walk closer to them. You may be lying to me." He motioned for the boy to go ahead while keeping his eye on the building.

The boy began to sniffle. "They're gonna kill me. I done figured it out. You the law, mister?"

"No, I'm just a citizen."

"You act like the law. Mister, I gotta piss."

"Step over by the wall."

"I really got to."

"Pee there."

"All right. All right. You don't know them two, do you?"

Slocum stared at the house right on the dirt sidewalk. "I'm fixing to meet them."

"What if they kill us?"

He shook his head. "I won't let them. Get behind me."

He could hear a woman crying and someone slapping her. "Shut your damn mouth," a gruff voice ordered.

"Oh, dear mother of God . . ." the boy began whispering. "Let me go."

"No. I'll protect you. Will you do what I say?"

"Oh, yeah, but I don't want to die."

"Then keep quiet."

A man with a pistol in his hand stepped out with his back to them not twenty steps away to search the street.

"Drop it!" Slocum ordered, and the man whirled around, not obeying his command. He shot in the direction of Slocum's voice.

The Colt barked loudly in Slocum's hand, and the bullet slammed into the man standing against the door. He fell down and Slocum knew the outlaw was hit hard enough in the chest to kill him. The sound of someone running out the back made him charge to the doorway but the dead man's body in the space forced him to jump over it. He saw the wet red face of Mrs. Briscoe with her hands tied behind her back, sitting at a table in the room.

"Cut her loose," he shouted to the boy as he ran hard for the back door. A wide-eyed man with a pistol, mounted on an unruly brown horse, was trying to rein him around. He took a wild shot at Slocum that raised dust where the lead struck the adobe wall. Slocum took aim, fired, and knew by the way the man ducked in the saddle that he was hit. But his mount tore away and the wounded kidnapper disappeared down the alley toward a side street.

"Kid, go see if he fell off his horse. I hit him."

"Yes sir." And he ran out the back door.

"You all right?" Slocum asked, going to Mrs. Briscoe, pained by the sight of her black eye and appearance.

"Where's Samuel?" Untied, she fell into his arms.

"Sam's doing great with a lady who's caring for him. We're going over there next."

"He never fell off the horse, sir," the boy reported.

"Thanks. What do I owe you?"

"Twenty dollars. I showed you right where she was at."

"You did well." Turning to Joan Briscoe, he explained, "He returned the livery buggy they'd rented, then he led me up here."

Slocum paid him and the boy bit on the coin.

"It isn't fake." Slocum scowled at him.

"You can't take no chances these days."

"You go back to Jenkins and tell him I need to rent a rig. And bring it over here on the double." He could hear a police whistle blowing and the bells of a paddy wagon en route to their location. More damn explaining to do.

"You're sure Sam's fine?" Her hand about squeezed his arm off.

Four policemen armed with clubs arrived, aided by a number of Mexican women pointing toward the adobe shack.

"What the hell was the shooting about?" the leader in his blue uniform demanded. One of his men squatted down and examined the dead man.

"He's dead, Sarge."

"Did you shoot him?" he asked Slocum.

"Yes sir, after he shot at me. Smell the pistol in his hand. It was shot at me only a few minutes ago. I returned fire in self-defense."

One of the officers jerked the dead man's gun out of his hand. Two others smelled it and agreed that it had been fired.

"This your gun?" one of the others asked, reaching out to take Slocum's pistol.

"No, sir. I borrowed it from Mr. Jenkins over at the livery. I knew I'd need the weapon to recover Mrs. Briscoe, who they kidnapped at the train depot yesterday."

"How did you find them?"

"That's a long story that I'll tell you at the police station. Send an officer with me. Mrs. Briscoe's son is with a babysitter that I hired. He's six months old. I was at your police headquarters this morning and explained all of this. Let us go get her baby boy first, and then I'll come directly to the station. I won't do anything else."

"Who is this corpse?" another asked.

"I never saw him before he came out that doorway and shot at me."

"Anyone know him?" their leader asked the onlookers. No answer.

"There's a wanted poster on him down at the station," the shortest policeman informed them.

"Cadrey knows them all," the leader said then took off his hat and turned to Mrs. Briscoe. "I'm sorry, ma'am, my bad manners. Someone has your boy?"

"I left Sam with Slocum for just a minute, went inside the train depot to use the facilities, and this dead man and another grabbed me. They beat me up and threatened to kill me. I still don't understand anything about it."

"I'm sorry, ma'am."

"Whose buckboard is that?"

The boy and buckboard had just rattled up.

Slocum told him, "I sent that boy for it so we could go get her son."

The man gave a big sigh. "Only for the lady would I do this. Irwin, go with them and take them to get her son. Then—"

"Let her check into a hotel, too. She's not going to run away. I'll go back with the officer, and the boy can tend the buckboard for me."

The sergeant, as if overwhelmed by all that had happened, finally agreed. He began giving orders to his men. "Load the dead man in the wagon and take it to the morgue. Cadrey, you and Reynolds talk to all the neighbors and find out about these men then look up the landlord.

"Slocum, you go check her into the hotel, get the baby in whatever order, and I'll meet you at the station when you get through."

Slocum helped Mrs. Briscoe up beside the boy. "Take us to this address." He showed him the paper it was written on.

"I can't read," the boy said.

"It's 54 Second Avenue." He joined the policeman on the tailgate and shook his head.

"We need to get our things from the depot, too," Slocum told him.

The cop nodded. "That was some shooting you did back there. He was drilled right in the heart. You killed many men?"

"No more than needed it." Slocum turned to speak to Joan, who was on the seat as the iron wheels turned up the light dust. "You all right, ma'am?"

"Yes, Slocum. Are you sure my boy is all right?"

"He's fine. We'll be there in a minute."

When they arrived at the babysitter's house, she quickly opened the door and smiled. "I'm so glad to see you. This must be his mother. Sam is fine, although my goat's milk isn't as good as yours."

She led Joan inside, and soon she had her boy in her arms, hugging him tight. Slocum got the boy's bag and thanked the woman.

"Keep the money. You earned it."

"Thank you. You are so kind. Come see me whenever you're in town."

"He's fine," Joan said excitedly. Slocum carried out the boy's things.

Next, they went to the depot and got the rest of their things. At the Hotel San Carlos, he took her and the baby down from the seat and started inside.

"Tell them we're husband and wife," she whispered. "I'm shaking so badly inside, I'll need to hold on to you."

"After we check in, I'll come upstairs with you to get you settled," he said. "Then I'll be back as soon as I'm done at the police station. In the meantime, I'll order you a bath so you can clean up."

She agreed and hugged Sam tighter. The baby looked pleased to be back in her arms, too. Slocum kissed her on the forehead and then he registered them as man and wife. Mr. and Mrs. John Slocum.

A boy named Rick brought in their luggage and the

policeman helped. Then he drove them to the police station and watched the horses. The long interrogation proved that the men were wanted for various robberies, including suspicion they'd been involved in the Val Verde Bank robbery, which was listed as an eighty-thousand-dollar theft. James Briscoe had been one of the robbers.

Things were finally settled. The patrolman was to return Jenkins's pistol to him the next day. The dead man was Ulysses Crabtree of Lyman, Texas, wanted for several bank, stage, and store robberies. Slocum donated the reward to the San Antonio Police Widows' Fund. That sped things along. The wounded man that escaped was thought to be James E. Lansberry from Grapevine, Texas, also under many other assumed names and sought for dozens of crimes.

The desk sergeant shook Slocum's hand and for the fortieth time told him gunplay inside the city limits was prohibited. Slocum nodded. Then three news reporters cornered him, asking a thousand questions. He referred them to the man at the desk.

He told Rick he wanted him to go back to the livery and stay there. He'd send word when he wanted him to bring the rig and be ready to go somewhere—he was unsure when or where and gave him a dollar for a bath and a haircut so he could get himself a job.

"I ain't never had a real job before, mister."

"Well, look sharp and you might get one."

"Yes, sir. How are you getting back to the hotel? I'll take you and can you tell that pretty lady I'm glad she's all right."

"I'll do that," Slocum said, mounting the seat, and they went back uptown.

It was obvious to him that those two kidnappers thought Joan's late husband had given her some of the loot from a previous robbery. Where did the money go? If she could figure that out, she might be a lot better off than she was now. There was more to learn, and he had some time to spare. If she could recall even a few bits of information that her husband may have let slip, maybe they could find the loot.

15

At the hotel, as planned, Slocum joined Mrs. Briscoe in her room. Once inside she hugged him, crying on his shirt. He realized how trim her hips were and that her breasts were probably still tender, but he bet Sam had emptied them. Her boy was asleep in a crib the hotel had provided.

Wiping her eyes, she shook her head. "What would I have done without you?"

He began to kiss away her tears. "You'd have made it somehow. Tell me what they wanted from you."

"Money from some robbery they claimed that James was in on, and when they split up, he was supposed to have had it and they didn't get their share. I didn't even know he was an outlaw."

"Where were you living at the time?"

"At his folks' place. He was supposed to be buying cattle for a man named Phillips out at Junction. I never met Phillips."

"Could he have hidden it there?"

"Sure, but I don't know where to look."

"Where was the last place you lived together?"

166

"North of Fort Worth. We rented a place."

"Did he hide anything there you know about?"

"I have searched and searched my mind. I don't know what to do . . ."

He kissed her hard on the mouth, and gathered her in his arms. It was the thing to do at that moment. With wild abandon, she kissed him back. He soon whispered in her ear, "This is taking advantage of your situation. You know that, don't you?"

"Oh, hold me, love me. I'm so shaken by all this happening, I need to forget everything."

"I can do that. But I don't want you to feel any regrets when it's over."

"I won't. I wouldn't be back with my son tonight if not for you. I won't regret anything. Take me, Slocum. I'm not pretty. But I'm clean. I did take a bath and I so appreciate you excluding me from that police business." She began unbuttoning her nice dress.

He kissed her again. They shed clothing and she pulled the blankets and sheet back from the bed. Then at last she lay naked on the bed and moved back to make room for him, holding out her arms.

"Are you sore anyplace from them beating you?"

"No, no, I'll be fine—I just need to be held and loved."

He gently felt for the crease and soon his fingertips explored her vagina's opening. She widened her knees and he felt the lubrication flowing over his fingers. She'd be all right. His knees on the bed, he crawled on top of her and she pulled him down to kiss him. He wrapped his hand around his already full erection to gently push the head of his dick into her. The resistance of her muscular ring felt tight as he slowly pumped more of his shaft into her.

Her eyes squeezed shut, her mouth wide open, she moaned, deliriously caught up in the frenzy of their act. She raised her chin up so he was looking down on her smooth face. His pounding into her grew faster and her hips came up higher to receive more and more of his length inside her. The strained head of his hard-on was as deep as it could go. He was really beginning to work on her, grinding the coarse hair of their pubic regions against each other.

Lost in the whirlwind, they were caught up in the total act. His mouth soon flooded with saliva, he swallowed hard. His breath hurt, raging in and out of his chest, as he strained to drive in and out of her tight box. He soared to wonderful heights, and she was past the point of even knowing what was happening—or where she was. Suspended in the fierce awe of it all, he knew his dick grew closer to an explosion, and when it came, she felt the surging warm liquid invade her body, washing away all her tension. Afterward, she collapsed into a never-never land of healing and satisfied sleep.

Sam's crying woke him up. Naked as Eve, Joan was nursing him on her left breast, sitting up cross-legged on the bed. His mother's comforting smile and warm milk made the baby close his eyes and think about going back to sleep.

"How's the little man doing?" Slocum asked, propping himself up on his elbows and wondering what they should do next.

"Fine, he's simply hungry. He never woke up last night. Kind of like his momma—done in. And I thought my wild honeymoon was something. It was a firecracker compared to last night's sky rockets, but you cleared my mind. I also thought of something. He gave me a key one time. He said for me to never lose it." She shook her head then swept her long curls back. "Now why in the hell did he give me that key? We had no locks to open."

"Where is it?" Slocum scooted out of bed and pulled his pants on.

"In the top tray of that jewelry box."

He unsnapped the two latches of the box and looked though some small trinkets, then found the key on a leather cord. He turned the key over and saw the engraving: SANB 30I.

With a headshake, he ran the edge of his upper teeth over his lower lip. "You know what this is?"

"No idea."

"It's the key to a safe-deposit box at the San Antonio National Bank."

"What for? We never had anything to keep there. Oh . . ." Her mouth fell open. "Could it be what those kidnappers wanted?"

"I have a strong idea it might be." His heart skipped a couple of beats. It just might be what they wanted.

"How do we get it?"

"We may need a lawyer to fill out some papers unless he has your name on the account."

"I never signed anything at a bank."

"Maybe he put it in both of your names. Then you could sign to get in there."

"What then?"

"We go in there and be very polite. If they let us in and unlock the box, we need to have some carpetbags to haul whatever is in there out—maybe."

"Sam, you may be rich yet," she said to her baby. Then she shook her head, looking very deep in thought. "Does it have to be returned?"

"I doubt any bank could identify it as their money. For all you know, he made it driving cattle up to Abilene, Kansas. The route's been changed, and the cattle shipping point is Wichita now so there'd be no records to check up there."

"Will there be more men like those two that want a share?"

"Who knows? We better see if we can get into the box first before we worry about that devil."

"Let's get something to eat. I'm starved," she suggested.

"Then take a taxi to the bank," Slocum said.

"What about your boy, Rick?"

"He's fine where he is for now. I wonder how those two knew to meet that train and grab you. That bothers me worse. Who did you tell you were coming back here?"

"I wrote his folks, Henry and Ida. They're out at Fredericksburg. I also wrote my folks up at Mason that I was coming home on the train this week and would ride the mail buckboard out to them. They probably told folks in town that I was coming home and when."

"So lots of people knew. That may be the answer. We'll get dressed and go see the banker."

"It will take me a little while to get ready." She looked concerned like it might upset him.

"That's fine. I'll go find us some food and coffee."

He dressed and went downstairs. She was hurrying around when he returned with steaming cups of coffee and some pastries. With a brush in her hand, she fixed her hair. "I'm shaking inside about this deal. I never saw a key for one of those before. It's a thin, cheap-looking key, too."

Then she put down the brush and looked hard at him. "When do you have to leave here?"

"Oh, I have a few weeks before I need to leave."

"Good. What if I break down at the bank?"

"You'll be fine. Eat some food and drink the coffee. I'll be there with you."

She began to dress. "My heavens, I'm still shaking from last night. That was wonderful."

"For me, too." He picked up Sam, who was uncomfortable about something. The boy grinned and he rocked him. "You're lucky, Joan. He's a fine boy."

She squeezed his arm. "Thank you. I'm so lucky you came along. Otherwise, I wouldn't have Sam or—"

His finger on her mouth silenced her. "There's no need to thank me. Just get yourself ready to sweet-talk the banker."

She nodded. "All right."

"Bring your marriage license, if you have it. We may need that as proof, and we may need a lawyer yet, too, but we'll deal with that later if we have to."

"Sure I have one." She went to her trunk and found the marriage license, then slid it into her small purse. Her shoes on, she stood up and took Sam. "I hope I'm ready."

"You look nice."

"Thank you, I don't know how I can, but let's go."

The taxi ride to the bank seemed too brief to her. The man at the bank, who was stiff and unfriendly, took the key and examined it. He handled it like it was piece of dried cow dung, then handed it back to her. He looked up the records and asked her if she was Mrs. Joan Briscoe.

"Yes, I am. I have my wedding certificate." She handed it to him as she and Slocum sat down in the visitors' chairs. "My husband has gone to Kansas. Mr. Slocum is a family friend helping me today."

"Nice to meet you, sir."

"The same."

Then the banker said, "Let's go back and I shall open the box for you."

Slocum saw the disgust in the man's eyes when he glanced at Sam. Hell, that kid won't do anything to your vault, Slocum thought.

They filed behind him into a room containing brass boxes. Hundreds of them. He used both his own master and her key and told them they could remove the box. It was a large vault box and Slocum pulled it out and placed it on the table in the room for them to examine.

Slocum thanked him and waited until he was gone before he opened the top. There were thousands of dollars neatly packed inside. He took a handful out and put them in her purse. She looked so pale, he feared she might faint.

"What do we do now?" she managed to ask quietly.

"We close the box and lock it. You put the key around

your neck. We walk out, thank him, and tell him you'll be back."

"How much is in there?"

"He left you and Sam a fortune is all I can say."

"I'm trembling inside."

"Buck up, girl. That's your money. It's safe in there even if they make a run on the bank. You have your name on that card now as the other box holder, so you can come back anytime you need to draw money out. No one else can."

"How much do I have in my purse?"

"A thousand, I figure."

"What will I do with it?"

"I'm taking you up to your folks' place or his. Your choice. San Antonio is too tough a place for a rich woman without a husband. You can get your life together again. Find a decent man."

She looked around the room to be certain they were alone. She shifted Sam in her arms, then leaned over to kiss Slocum. "I am so excited, my heart may explode."

"Mine, too."

At Price's Livery, Rick came running out. "What now?"

"We're going on a trip to her folks' house up in Mason. You're going to drive the buckboard."

"Can I . . ." Joan chewed on her lip as if hesitant.

"What?" Slocum asked.

"I want to buy my mother a kitchen range and have it sent up there. Can I do that?"

He smiled. "Hell, darling, you can do anything you want to do. Today I'm buying you a better buckboard and two good horses, plus me a saddle horse. We need our things from the hotel. Sam needs more diapers. What else?"

"You got a job for me?" Rick asked.

"Of course. We're taking you along as my driver." Joan tousled his freshly cut hair. "You're my employee now."

"Yes, ma'am."

The deal was made for a team of sharp bay horses and a new buckboard, and for Slocum a nice four-year-old sorrel gelding to ride. At Hanson Brothers, a large hardware store downtown, Joan bought her mother a fancy chrome-trimmed kitchen range. They promised to deliver it to her folks' ranch in a week. Then they bought food, diapers, clothing, a felt hat for Rick, and a few other supplies.

Before sunup, they left in the loaded buckboard with Rick driving and Slocum on his new sorrel. The trip required three days and they reached her parents' place in the late afternoon of the third day.

With the dogs barking and raising hell, her gray-haired mother, her hair in a bun, came running out of the ranch house. She'd never seen Sam, and was she ever excited to hold him!

A tall, slightly stoop-shouldered man in his late forties rode up on a good ranch horse, and shook Slocum's hand. "Ben Coats is my name."

"Slocum is mine and the boy on the seat is Rick. He's the driver."

"Where's her man?"

Slocum leaned over. "That's a long story. She can tell you the details, but he's dead."

"Oh, my heavens, that's a shame. We'll sorely miss him. And who might you be?"

"I'm just a friend helping her and Sam. She can tell you the rest."

"Nice team and rig," Ben said, admiring it. "I don't know many widow women who can afford that nice an outfit."

Slocum agreed and took off his hat to meet her mother, Fel—for Felicia, which she never used.

Ben showed him and the boy where to put up the horses. He stood and admired the buckboard with his chin in his hand and then he said again, "That is one fine rig."

After a wonderful supper and lots of explaining, Ben showed Rick his room in the barn. Slocum took his war bag, his bedroll, and Joan's things up to her small house on the hill. The two of them were listening to the frogs chirp while standing on the front porch, and he wondered how her parents would take to him staying with her.

"What will they think, especially your mother, about us staying together up here?"

"She understands that I've been through a lot and knows I owe you for all you've done for me and Sam."

"You don't—"

Her finger silenced him. "Quit acting like you never did anything. I can't wait until that range gets here. I guess Dad was shocked about the horses and buckboard, wasn't he?"

"He knew they cost a pretty penny."

"What will you do now?"

He hugged her in the fading light after sundown. "Take you to bed."

She gave him a squeeze. "Good. I really need that."

The next morning Slocum rode into town and asked around about the two men, Crabtree and Lansberry, who'd kidnapped Mrs. Briscoe. The marshal, Ike Benton, said they were newcomers and that they weren't worth too much, but he never expected them to be outlaws like that. They'd been hanging around town a lot the week before, and Slocum figured that was how they'd heard about her returning by train.

"I shot Lansberry in San Antonio," Slocum said, "so he's wounded, but he fled and the police down there want him."

"I'll be sure he gets delivered to them," the marshal said. "If I can find him."

"Mrs. Briscoe will pay you a reward for doing that."

"Thanks. I can use some money."

"I figured so." Slocum shook his hand and started back for the ranch on his new horse, Red.

"Hey," someone shouted at him.

He turned in the saddle and saw Jim Davis riding up the street on a good roan ranch horse.

"What are you doing here in Mason?" Slocum asked.

"Looking for you. Schade said you'd come up here."

"Did you get married?"

"No. Aw, hell, I should have known she wouldn't. She ran out before our wedding. Too much damn country here for her. She's a city girl. What are you up to?"

"I'm helping a widow woman."

"Who's that, and how did you get tangled up with her?"

"Long story. Let's go have a few beers and I'll tell you all about her."

After his abbreviated tale, and a few draft beers, he asked Jim what he'd do next.

"Hell, I don't know. I guess I'll find me some hardworking German girl and settle down."

"I ain't shoving her off, but Joan is a nice woman. I can't stay here. I explained that to her already." He wouldn't mention her money. Jim could find that out in time. He had a quick thought that maybe Jim was a loser, but no, he was a sincere guy who'd take good care of his family. Jim couldn't help the fact that the woman he'd picked before didn't want to be a rancher's wife.

"You don't mind if I come by and meet her?"

"No, I'm out of here in a week or so if Lansberry doesn't show up."

"What if I found him? Would that impress her, do you think?"

"I think it would, but be careful. He's a killer."

"I will. I can find him if anyone can."

They shook hands and parted company.

Back at Joan's place that night, Slocum told her about Jim and what a good man he was.

"He's not an outlaw, too, is he?" she asked, lying naked and half-sprawled on his chest.

"No. He wants to settle down and run his father's ranch."

She looked warily at him in the room's dull light. "He'd have big boots to fill with me."

"Simply meet him. He's honest."

"I guess I'll need someone. And I do have the money to build a ranch. Why didn't James do that instead of robbing banks and getting himself killed?"

"Oh, people get into things then can't get out of them."

She pursed her lips and crawled up to kiss him. Soon they were making furious love, knowing it was one of their last times together.

Two days later on a lathered horse, Jim Davis rode in about sunup while the two of them were eating breakfast at her house.

Rick brought him up to her place on the run, and by the time they got there, they were both out of breath.

"I found that other kidnapper," Jim said. "He's shacked up down on the Pertinales River."

"I'll saddle my horse." Slocum stood up.

"No, I can do that," Rick said. "Should I load your bed-roll?"

"Thanks. Joan, this is my friend Jim Davis."

Jim took off his hat and nodded. She beamed at him and gave him her hand to shake. "He's told me a lot about you."

"Ma'am, he's a great guy. I sure appreciate meeting you."

"Drop by again, Jim."

"Oh, yes, ma'am. I sure will do that. My ranch is over the hill about twenty miles, but I'll be back if that's okay?"

"That will be fine, Mr. Davis."

"No Mr. Davis, please, ma'am. I'm just Jim."

"Good, I'm just Joan."

"Yes, ma'am. I mean Joan." He put on his hat.

"He'll be back for his reward anyway." Slocum laughed.

He felt sure those two might make it if he was out of the picture. Rick and Jim went outside while Slocum said good-bye.

"I know. When you get Lansberry, you won't come back—you already told me you couldn't stay in one place too long and why." She motioned toward the front door with a toss of her head. "Is he as good as he looks?"

"Yes. Remember, that money came from a cattle drive to Abilene, and it was your husband's intention to buy a ranch with it."

"I know. No one can prove otherwise. Thanks," she said, and kissed him.

As he walked toward the door, she called out, "Wait," then reached for her purse. Taking out some large bills, she handed them to him. "Go with care, big man. You ever need anything, wire me."

"I will. Tell Sam when he grows up, I loved him, too."

She nodded and smiled through some tears.

Slocum and Jim mounted up and rode out to find their man. It would be a good day's ride down there. Damn, Slocum hated to leave her sweet body and disposition, but he wanted Jim to make it with her. He hoped it would work between them. She was a good person and so was Jim.

"She's a pretty woman," Jim said.

"Yes, she really is." Slocum glanced back then he turned forward. "How did you find Lansberry?"

"Riffraff knows where it's piled up. There's a guy down there named Gus Hailey who has a bad thirst for whiskey and knows every detail that happens in that country down there. Took a fifth over to his place and he told me all about Lansberry and where to find him."

"Good, I want him behind bars and this thing settled."

The next morning was cool and threatened rain. They wore their slickers sitting their horses in a grove of cedars and live oak. Wood smoke from a cookstove filled his nostrils.

"Reckon he'll come outside?" Jim asked.

"Any minute."

"When this is settled, are you going to meet that woman?" Jim asked.

"The one I got released from the insane ward?" Slocum smiled at him.

Jim laughed and shook his head. "Bet she's grateful, too."

"Anyone who wasn't nuts would become that way in one of those places."

"Was Proctor crazy?"

"He wanted it all to himself. Someone said he broke out of the Fort Worth jail. Don't know where he went to."

"They never got him?" Then Jim held out his hand. Someone was coming out of the back door and heading for the outhouse.

Slocum drew his rifle out of its scabbard. He levered a shell in the chamber and they rode their horses in closer. Their man was already inside the privy. "Lansberry, get out here with your hands up."

"Who the hell are you?" he called through the wooden door of the outhouse.

"The law. You're under arrest for kidnapping Mrs. Briscoe."

"Fuck you!" A pistol shot and gun smoke came from the outhouse.

Slocum slammed two rifle bullets into the side of the outhouse and the man fell out of the structure's door to the ground.

A Mexican woman ran from the house toward him, but Jim cut her off with his horse.

"Get out of my way!" she screamed in Spanish, cursing him in her native language.

Slocum jumped off his own horse, felt for the man's pulse. Nothing. He used the rifle butt to push himself to his feet. "He's dead."

The woman began to cry and curse them. Slocum

shoved the rifle in the scabbard and remounted, ignoring her loss.

"That settles that," Jim said, satisfied. "I'll go tell Mrs. Briscoe for you that this one is dead and won't bother her again."

Slocum looked over at him and nodded. "Good luck. Joan is a fine young woman. See you, Jim." Then he rode off. It was still a far piece to Galveston. He had better move on.

He stood in the stirrups and looked back to check that his war bag and bedroll were secure. She'd given him over five hundred dollars, and it was safe inside his pocket. What luck. He had a good horse, too.

16

The sea breeze swept off Galveston Bay and covered Slocum's face. There was a slightly fishy smell in his nose. The vessels in the harbor, with their anchors down, sat on the gentle sea. Gulls screamed and landed in flocks to scavenge whatever they could. Several people were on the beach. He'd stabled his horse at a livery, had the hustler wash Red down and grain him as well. The trip down had worked the sorrel hard, and he wanted him in good shape whenever he left this place.

He had taken a room at Galveston's finest, the Bressler Hotel, and was expecting her arrival at any time. There was a letter waiting for him at the desk when he arrived. The paper was scented with expensive perfume, which made it seem like she'd almost materialized in his hands while he was reading the flowery script.

Dear John—

I will leave Santa Fe on the eighth and take the stage to Texas. The train from El Paso should shuttle me

*rapidly to San Antonio, then down to Galveston in
a few days. My darling, I can hardly wait. Elania is
married to Fred Golden and is almost back to her
old self. Katrina and her son are settled in at the
main house. She still does not talk, but she smiles
more. The store business is growing again. I have
three new men in charge of the divisions so I can
leave here and lounge with you and not worry about
the situation.*

*So rest your wonderful body and I will be there
shortly.*

With love, Camilla

He went into the hotel bar and had a beer. He spoke to
a lovely woman from France who asked him in her heavily accented voice, "Are you really a cowboy?"

"I have been."

"Oh, how nice. Are you here with someone?"

"Regretfully, she is on her way here." He smiled as she
swept away, making a *tsk-tsk* sound with her tongue.

Then Camilla arrived. He was reading a Houston newspaper seated in the lobby when someone walked up to him
and simply stood there until he felt her presence and the
scent of her perfume reached his nose.

"How are you?" he asked her, setting the paper aside
and rising to kiss her.

"Much better." Her smile signaled his future adventures.

He kissed her long and hard. When he released her, she
acted like she had been drinking, then she laughed.

"My head is spinning. I've been on the road a week,
and I am so—so glad to be here. Elania sends you her
love—and her thanks."

He took her arm. "Your luggage is here?"

"Sent to our room."

"We better go check on it."

Linked arm in arm, they headed for the stairs. The party was about to begin. And he was ready.

"You'll be glad to hear my late husband was killed by some renegade Indians."

"Proctor is dead?"

"Yes. After he escaped the Fort Worth authorities, he was killed in an Indian attack on a stagecoach he took from Lordsburg to Tucson. They think some Indian chief named *Ger-on-i-mo* led them."

"Never heard of him."

"Neither had I. But Fred says that will settle all our legal problems."

He stopped climbing the stairs, pulled her into his arms, and kissed her thoroughly.

"That was nice," she said, smiling, when he released her. Then on the move again, she asked coyly over her shoulder, "How soon can I get another kiss from you?"

Slocum laughed. He knew he'd laugh a lot in her company, and he needed to. He'd been through hell since that day when he'd come out of a dust storm, then a snowstorm, and arrived at Gill McKee's fort up on Cap Rock.

"Try and stop me," he said, kissing her all the way to their room.

Watch for

**SLOCUM AND THE YELLOWSTONE
SCOUNDREL**

411th novel in the exciting SLOCUM series
from Jove

Coming in May!

GIANT-SIZED ADVENTURE FROM
AVENGING ANGEL LONGARM.

BY TABOR EVANS

2006 Giant Edition:

LONGARM AND THE
OUTLAW EMPRESS

2007 Giant Edition:

LONGARM AND
THE GOLDEN EAGLE
SHOOT-OUT

2008 Giant Edition:

LONGARM AND THE
VALLEY OF SKULLS

2009 Giant Edition:

LONGARM AND THE
LONE STAR TRACKDOWN

2010 Giant Edition:

LONGARM AND THE
RAILROAD WAR

2013 Giant Edition:

LONGARM AND
THE AMBUSH AT HOLY
DEFIANCE

penguin.com/actionwesterns

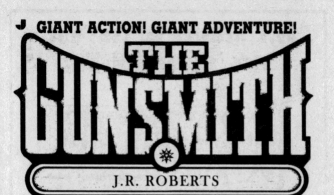

GIANT ACTION! GIANT ADVENTURE!

THE GUNSMITH

J.R. ROBERTS

Little Sureshot and
the Wild West Show
(Gunsmith Giant #9)

Red Mountain
(Gunsmith Giant #11)

The Marshal from Paris
(Gunsmith Giant #13)

Andersonville Vengeance
(Gunsmith Giant #15)

Dead Weight
(Gunsmith Giant #10)

The Knights of Misery
(Gunsmith Giant #12)

Lincoln's Revenge
(Gunsmith Giant #14)

The Further Adventures
of James Butler Hickok
(Gunsmith Giant #16)

penguin.com/actionwesterns

M455AS0812

1716

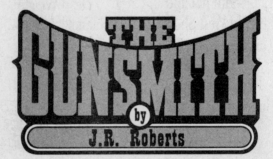